Vlas Mikhailovich DOROSHEVICH (1864-1922) was an outstanding writer whose vast and varied journalistic output included travel accounts, satirical pieces, theatrical reviews and court reporting. His early efforts, light pieces for humorous magazines, were influenced by Saltykov-Shchedrin. Satire remained his life-long love.

Later he travelled extensively in Europe, North America and Asia, writing articles on the life of ordinary people in the countries he visited and on the wider issues affecting them. Politically Doroshevich was on the left, and his socialist leanings are reflected in his writings.

Through his travels he became interested in folktales and collected them enthusiastically. Indeed, Doroshevich is best remembered today for his pastiche folktales and legends. Although their satire was ostensibly directed at the autocracy and bureaucracy in the Orient, readers were not slow to realize their application to life in tsarist Russia. Not surprisingly, the censors often stopped publication of those periodicals that published them. Doroshevich's tales remain highly relevant to this day.

GLAS NEW RUSSIAN WRITING

contemporary Russian literature

in English translation

Volume 53

Vlas Doroshevich

What the Emperor Cannot Do

Tales and Legends of the Orient

Translated by Rowen Glie
(in collaboration with Ronald M. Landau)
and John Dewey

glas
MOSCOW

GLAS Publishers
tel./fax: +7(495)441-9157
perova@glas.msk.su
www.glas.msk.su

DISTRIBUTION

In USA and CANADA
Consortium Book Sales and Distribution
1094 Flex Drive
Jackson, TN 38301-5070
tel: 800-283-3572; fax: 800-351-5073
orderentry@perseusbooks.com

In the UK
CENTRAL BOOKS
orders@centralbooks.com
www.centralbooks.com
Direct orders: INPRESS
tel: 0191 230 8104
customerservices@inpressbooks.co.uk
www.inpressbooks.co.uk

Within Russia
Jupiter-Impex
www.jupiterbooks.ru

Editors: Natasha Perova & Joanne Turnbull
Camera-ready copy: Tatiana Shaposhnikova
Front cover: Detail from Vassily Vereschagin's *Doors of Tamerlane*

ISBN 978-5-7172-0094-3

CONTENTS

INDIAN TALES

The Russian King of the Feuilleton

Vlas Mikhailovich Doroshevich
(1864 - 1922)

Doroshevich was one of Russia's most popular and widely read writers in his day, mostly known for his book about the Sakhalin labor camps, for his theater reviews, satirical essays about the Tsarist bureaucracy, and acerbic social lampoons. When this "King of the Feuilleton", as he was widely known, contributed a story to a newspaper, circulation doubled. His parables stylized as Oriental tales are timeless. They sound as topical today as they did in Doroshevich's time.

Doroshevich was born in the Ryazan province, where his mother Alexandra Sokolova was a member of the wealthy upper classes. She was educated at the prestigious Smolny Institute in St. Petersburg, but was disinherited by her family for marrying Vlas's father, an unsuccessful writer who was far beneath her socially. He died shortly before Vlas was born.

When Vlas was six months old, Alexandra, in trouble with the police as a political nihilist and struggling financially, left him in a cheap hotel room with a note in French saying: "The child has not yet been christened. Please call him Blaise in honor of Blaise Pascal." The boy was adopted by a kindly childless couple by the name of Doroshevich who Russianized the boy's name. Ten years later Alexandra, now a relatively successful author, went to court to try and regain custody of Vlas. The litigation dragged on for nearly ten years during which she kept kidnapping her son from his adoptive parents, who in turn stole him back. When the Dorosheviches finally had a child of their own, they gave up the fight for Vlas.

At the age of sixteen, Vlas had to start earning his living. He withdrew from school (he was about to be expelled for "impertinence") and tried various jobs: he worked as a tutor, a digger, a laborer, a proofreader and an actor. At seventeen he began writing for newspapers, including *Moskovsky Listok* (Moscow Newsletter) and *Volna* (Wave), under the pen name "Merry Muscovite". He was often homeless and constantly starving, but determined to become a real writer like his idols: Gogol, Griboyedov, and Saltykov-Shchedrin.

His publisher, the famous Ivan Sytin, used to tell the story of how in the winter of 1880, a schoolboy shivering with cold had come into his office and requested to speak to the director. Intrigued, Sytin received him. The boy had brought the manuscript of a short novel (a popular rewrite of Gogol's tale "A Terrible Vengeance") and wanted fifteen rubles for it, no more and no less. "But why aren't you in school?" Sytin asked.

"Yesterday," replied Doroshevich, "I was expelled. During lessons I wrote anecdotes about my teachers. I got caught and was expelled. Now I must have fifteen rubles." Sytin bought the story and launched Doroshevich's writing career.

During the 1880s, he became a skillful journalist and critic, writing for popular papers such as *Razvlechenie* (Entertainment), *Peterburgsky Listok* (St. Petersburg Newsletter), and *Budilnik* (Alarm Clock), which also employed the young Anton Chekhov. They became friends and Chekhov remained a moral model for Doroshevich throughout his life. "Chekhov is a symbol of truth for me," he said.

In 1893 Doroshevich moved to Odessa to work on the *Odessky Listok* (Odessa Newsletter), a local liberal paper with a large circulation. On assignment in France, he was influenced by the feuilleton style of journalism. He developed his own writing style along those lines: short straight-to-the-point sentences, biting as a whip. He made a name with his brilliant satirical sketches of local officials, unmasked the predatory and inhuman nature of Russian business, and laughed at their petty-bourgeois way of life and thinking.

In 1897, seven years after Chekhov, Doroshevich traveled to the island of Sakhalin, off the east coast of Siberia, to write about the Tsarist labor camps there. It was part of his personal mission to defend the rights of ordinary people and to disprove the then current belief that suffering works as a catharsis of the soul. The climate of the island was most severe, and the condition of the prisoners terrible. He recorded his experiences and impressions in his book *Sakhalin* (now published in English translation by the UK Anthem Press as *Russia's Penal Colony in the Far East.*) The first Sakhalin stories, published in *Odessky Listok,* caused severe problems with the censorship. Doroshevich ended by having to leave the paper, and Odessa. When the book came out in 1903 it was banned by the Tsarist government and removed from all the libraries.

In 1897-98 Doroshevich also traveled in the East, the inspiration for his "Legends and Tales of the Orient". These tales first appeared in periodicals and then in 1902 were collected in a book, also called *Legends and Tales of the Orient.* (In the USSR the book was published once, in 1983, in a limited edition by a Science Publishers in Minsk, and not yet reprinted to this day.)

In 1899, Doroshevich became coeditor with Alexander Amfiteatrov of the liberal paper *Rossia.* Within three years the paper had been closed down for its lampoons of the top bureaucracy and the imperial family. Sytin now put Doroshevich in charge of his paper *Russkoe Slovo* (Russian Word) and before long circulation had climbed to a record 1,000,000 readers, the highest in the land. Doroshevich's brilliant investigative journalism irritated bureaucrats, who referred to him derisively as "the second counsel for the prosecution", "the fourth judge" and "the thirteenth juror".

Nevertheless, Doroshevich succeeded on several occasions in getting an unjust verdict reversed. He remained editor of *Russkoe Slovo* until 1918 when the Soviets closed it down.

Doroshevich published his best known work *The Way of the Cross (Krestny Put')*, in October 1915. It is an account of the refugees from the German invasion of Russia during World War I. He journeyed from Moscow in his own automobile to meet the oncoming refugees, travelling through to the rear of the Russian army and recording the hardships and struggles he witnessed along the way. When people died by the roadside, they put up crosses to mark the burial sites, hence the title of his account, *The Way of the Cross*.

Doroshevich was not a Socialist and never belonged to any political party. But as a man with a warm heart and a sharp mind, he hated injustice and cruelty, the servility of the weak and poor, and the insolence of the strong and rich. Doroshevich could not stand tyranny in any form while meek acceptance of tyranny made him livid.

Though a wealthy man by 1917, he welcomed the rise of the Bolsheviks and the Russian Revolution. This may have been partly due to his status as an outcast among bourgeois-minded intellectuals, whom he often lampooned in his satirical pieces. However, Doroshevich was soon bitterly disappointed in the new Soviet rule. The oppression of the Soviets turned out to be no less severe than that under Tsarism.

In 1918, after *Russkoe Slovo* was closed down, Doroshevich went to the Crimea for a cure, travelling through the civil war-ravaged country. The last years of his life were for Doroshevich a slow dying process: he was ruined physically, morally, and financially. In 1920 he came across his own obituary in the *Literary Herald* and wrote to the editors: "Dear Editors, with very warm feelings I read my obituary in your paper. Everything in it is true except for one sentence: I am not dead. This news happens to be premature. I apologize for being very much alive and wish the same to all of you. Salute et fraternite. The late Vlas Doroshevich."

Written more than a century ago, *Tales and Legends of the Orient* could have been created by and for the modern, rebellious youth of today — the anti-establishment feeling being obviously universal and timeless. Fairytales permitted Doroshevich to talk openly about the many wrongs that could not be discussed in any newspaper article. In his fairytales Doroshevich availed himself of complete freedom to mock, to despise, and to accuse the great, the strong, and the rich for their wickedness, hypocrisy, stupidity, and indifference to the ones they hurt so much.

Doroshevich's tales are a mixture of pure fantasy, irony, and often despair caused by the fact that between men in power living in their ivory towers and the people they rule over there is a corrupt bureaucracy – an "establishment". Any effort by a man in power – an "Emperor of China" or a "Caliph" – is always thwarted by his own "establishment" created to execute his orders. The "Emperor" or "Caliph" themselves are kept so far from reality by their underlings that the most obvious solution to any problem often escapes them. Any chance for a better solution devised by the ruler himself or his corrupt "establishment" results in greater suffering for the very people the decree was supposed to help. Whatever their subject, these tales are unexpected, exciting, colorful, and supremely readable.

This GLAS edition of Doroshevich's tales is the first English edition of these parables for all times and all lands. They have lost nothing of their relevance, alas, and readers today will surely be able to appreciate the wit and humor of this forgotten classic from the turn of the 20th century.

The Editors

Chinese Tales

What the Emperor Cannot Do

From the *Hundred Golden Fairy Tales*
read to the future Emperor in childhood

The Omnipotent Emperor saw all kinds of people at court, mostly clever and cunning people. One day he had a wish to see happy people as well. "I am the sun that gilds only the tops of the mountains while the rays never reach the valleys," he said to himself, whereupon he ordered his Master of Ceremonies to bring him a list of officials of the lowest grade.

The Master of Ceremonies brought him 666 scrolls, each one 66 cubits long, hardly enough for all the names.

"Goodness!" said the Emperor. "There are so many of them!" And pointing to the name of Tun Li, a mandarin of the 48th class, he said to his Master of Ceremonies, "Find out what kind of a man he is!"

The orders of the Emperor were always carried out immediately. Therefore, before the Emperor could count to 10,000, the Master of Ceremonies returned and, bowing low, said, "This is your old servant, O Omnipotent Son of Heaven. He is an honest and meek official, a good husband and father. He lives happily with his wife and he has raised his daughter in piety and diligent work."

"Let joy be his fate!" said the Emperor. "I want to bring

him bliss with the look of my eyes. Go and tell him that on the first day of the new moon he can present himself to me with his entire family."

"He will die of happiness!" exclaimed the Master of Ceremonies.

"Let us hope that this will not happen," smiled the good Emperor. "Go and carry out my order."

When the Master of Ceremonies returned to the palace the Emperor asked:

"And what did he say?"

"Your sacred wish has been fulfilled, O Omnipotent Son of Heaven!" said the Master of Ceremonies, prostrating himself before the Emperor. "Your gracious command was conveyed to Tun Li with a roar of drums, the sounds of pipes, and the people's praise for your wisdom!"

"And what did Tun Li say?" asked the Emperor.

"He seemed to become insane with happiness. Never has the world seen such mad joy!" was the reply.

The appointed day for Tun Li to present himself and his family to the Emperor was approaching too slowly — as is always the case when something is eagerly awaited — and the Emperor was becoming impatient. He wanted to look at the happy man as soon as possible, so one evening he dressed himself as a simple coolie and, accompanied by an escort, he went to the outskirts of Peking where Tun Li lived. Even from a great distance one could hear the shouting coming from the house of Tun Li.

"Do they exult so loudly?" asked the Emperor, and joy filled his heart.

"O you," cried Tun Li, "most miserable of all women, most contemptible of all beings on whom the sun ever shone! I curse the day when I decided to marry you. Truly evil dragons put the idea into my head!"

"For 300 moons we have lived as husband and wife," said Tun Li's tearful wife, "and never have I heard such curses. You always said I was a kind, good and loyal wife. You praised me."

"Yes! But we did not have to be presented to the Emperor!" Tun Li fumed. "You will cover me with shame. You will make me a laughingstock! Do you think that you will be able to make the 33 gracious bows required by etiquette? Humiliated by you and our daughter, I will have to hide myself in a dark hole. And our daughter! Here is the other most disgusting being in the whole world. Such ugliness the sun has never seen!"

"Father!" cried Tun Li's daughter, also in tears. "Did you not call me a beauty? My lovely My-Cian? Did you not say that there is no one in the whole world who is kinder, better, more obedient than I?"

"Yes! But your feet are two fingers too long," cried Tun Li in desperation. "I feel certain the Emperor will be horrified when he sees that monstrosity."

"I was not born to be carried in palanquins," cried poor My-Cian. "My feet are for walking. I'll have to marry a meek official like you, Father. I was raised to work."

"Cursed be your ugliness when one has to be presented to the Emperor," cried Tun Li, losing all control.

Just then the sound of a gong was heard and a usurer entered the room: "Now then Tun Li. What do you say to my conditions?"

"But we will die of hunger if we accept them," said Tun Li, covering his face in despair.

"As you wish," shrugged the usurer. "But remember, time is passing. If you wait too long there will be no time in which to make you a robe of blue silk with golden sleeves, a silk-embroidered robe for your wife, and a dress embroidered with flowers for your daughter. Everything that you must have to be presented at court. What will you do then?"

"Very well! I agree, I agree," muttered Tun Li.

"Good! But remember, so that we do not have an argument later: I will prepare all that you need, and every new moon you will bring me three quarters of your salary."

"But we will die from hunger," Tun Li cried. "Take half of it! Do not kill us!"

Tun Li, his wife, and little My-Cian fell down on their knees before the usurer, imploring him to take only half of Tun Li's salary. "Don't you see? We will have to starve all our lives."

"No!" insisted the usurer. "Three quarters of your salary every new moon! This is my last word. Take it or leave it! Yes or no?"

In tears, Tun Li replied, "Very well. Prepare all."

"Oh, Heaven," murmured the Emperor, and his eyes filled with tears.

"Don't you dare call me Omnipotent!" the Emperor cried when, upon returning to the palace, his Master of Ceremonies, according to protocol, prostrated himself before him and called him just that. "Don't you dare lie to me! What kind of omnipotence do I have if I cannot make a man happy?"

Later, while strolling with sadness in his heart in his magnificent fragrant gardens, the Emperor thought, "I am the sun that warms and shines only from afar and burns when it comes closer to the poor earth."

Translated by Rowen Glie

The Emperor's First Outing

Throughout his blessed life the Emperor San Yanki (may he be an example to us all!) had a particular passion for travelling and acquiring new knowledge.

All the same he reigned successfully for 242 moons[1] without ever seeing Peking. Certainly this was not for any lack of desire on his part.

Every day the Emperor would announce to his Prime Minister Zhuar Fucian: "Today I shall go out and see Peking."

The Prime Minister would bow low before the Emperor and scurry off to give the necessary orders.

The palace guards and musicians would appear, palanquins and banners would be assembled, and the mandarins would mount their horses.

The Prime Minister would report: "Everything has been prepared for the execution of your will, O Son of Heaven!"

And the Emperor would go to take his seat in the palanquin. At this point, however, something was always bound to happen.

It might be the Chief Astronomer emerging from the throng of courtiers to fall on his face and announce: "Ruler of the Universe, one minute from now the most fearful thunderstorm will break over Peking, bringing torrential rain and hailstones the size of the swallows' eggs of which Your Majesty is so fond. A terrible whirlwind will blind everyone, making it impossible to see. Any palanquin out in the streets at that moment would find itself in a most unenviable position. It would be blown into the air, spun around, swept

---

[1] 20 years and 2 months

up to the clouds and then hurled back to earth with such violence that of course anyone in it would not survive for an instant. Today this fearful hurricane will rage over the whole of Peking, except for your palace and gardens, which the Heavens themselves dare not assail. Thus it is written in the stars and recorded in our books, O Joy of the Universe."

Or the Court Historian might step forward, bow down before the Emperor and declare: "Master of the Earth! Permit me to remind you that today happens to be the anniversary of the death of your great ancestor Huar Zingzun, who lived twelve thousand moons ago, and that national tradition requires you to remain closeted in the palace on this day and, outwardly at least, to give yourself up to sorrowing."

Or again it might be the Chief Eunuch who would come running toward the Emperor, fling himself violently to the ground and announce: "Master of the Rivers, Seas and Mountains! A new slave girl has just been brought in, and never before have I witnessed such beauty! She is truly a flower, a freshly picked flower! It will be cause for regret if you delay seeing her even for an instant. Just come and look for yourself!"

And so the royal progress through Peking would be postponed.

When he had reigned auspiciously for 242 moons, however, and the 243rd had begun, the Emperor San Yanki declared: "Enough! This has gone too far! I know who is behind these machinations: that wily fox Zhuar Fucian! But do what he will, I shall see Peking, and that's that!"

After first paying some servants to ensure their loyalty, he said to them: "Strike the great gong used to proclaim the death of Emperors. Start wailing and lamenting as loud as you can. Call out: 'The Emperor is dead!' Tear your clothes and claw your faces. You will be paid for all of this."

Then he lay down on a high couch which the servants had prepared according to his instructions.

The servants did as he had bidden. They beat the great gong and announced to the courtiers who, their faces deathly pale, came running at the sound.

"The Light of the Sun has gone out; the Joy of the Universe is transformed to grief: the Fount of Wisdom, our Emperor, was dining when suddenly, in the middle of his meal, he passed away!"

The palace filled with lamentation and intrigue.

The Prime Minister groveled at the feet of San Yanki's successor, saying: "Son of Heaven, I will initiate you into all the complexities of governing the country. Put your trust in me!"

Tradition dictated that the first ceremony to be performed was the emptying of the 'basket of wishes' beside the Emperor's throne.

In fact there was only one slip of paper in it, and on this the deceased Emperor had recorded a single wish: "I wish to be buried on the same couch I shall be found lying on in the palace. Let no one dare to touch my body or even come near."

The wish of a deceased Emperor being sacred his instructions were duly followed.

He was carried to the imperial cemetery, borne aloft above the crowds on the same couch he had lain on in the palace. It was a magnificent, glittering procession, with everyone dressed in white.

The streets of Peking were thronged with people who had gathered to see the Emperor, even if he were dead, in the flesh.

The priests chanted, the courtiers sobbed, the ordinary folk made their remarks; while high above them all the

Emperor lay on his couch and, peeping through one half-open eye, observed Peking.

"Goodness, what pigs the Chinese are," he thought as he lay there looking at the city. "How can they live under those roofs with so many holes in them? Even then it wouldn't matter so much if they had warm clothing on in case it rains, yet they go about in rags and tatters. But listen: what is it they are shouting?"

Having seen as much as he wanted for the moment, he listened instead. The citizens of Peking were calling out: "Yah! You palace fox, Zhuar Fucian! Now there's an end to your robbing and pillaging! When the new Emperor cuts your head off, you'll have to go into the next life without it! And when it is put on display for public vilification, we shall spit on it! Never again shall you steal the clothes off our backs!"

"Aha! So that explains their raggedy appearance!" the Emperor thought to himself. "Just you wait, you villain!"

By this time the procession had reached the imperial cemetery. The people were sent away, leaving only the courtiers to stand at the graveside.

Roaring with laughter, the Emperor raised himself on his couch.

"Ha, ha, ha! Wasn't that an excellent joke I played on you all? Well, Zhuar Fucian, was there no hurricane during my tour of Peking?"

All the courtiers had turned pale, but palest of all was Zhuar Fucian. They were all trembling, yet it was Zhuar Fucian who trembled the most.

"What do you wish to do now?" he asked the Emperor.

"First of all," replied San Yanki, "I wish to return to the palace and reclaim my throne. After that we shall see."

Zhuar Fucian looked around helplessly at the other courtiers.

The Court Historian stepped forward. "That is out of the question!" he exclaimed. "We must live in accordance with the traditions of our ancestors. Yet no Emperor has ever died and then come back to life. This is quite unheard of. It could unleash the most fearful disasters and popular unrest on a vast scale. Quite frankly, it could mean the end of China itself!"

The First Master of Ceremonies also spoke up. "Quite out of the question!" he exclaimed. "Everything is governed by protocol, yet this is in complete breach of all protocol. What has been done cannot be undone: the funeral has taken place and, most importantly, the basket of wishes has been opened, which according to protocol may be done only after the death of an Emperor. Now it has been opened, quite clearly you are dead. In any case there is no form of protocol for the return of an Emperor from the cemetery to his throne. And who will observe the sacred laws in our country if we ourselves are the first to set protocol aside? That really could spell the end for China!"

"Indeed, the end of China, no less!" the Chief Priest also spoke up. "It is contrary to all the holy laws of our Heavenly religion. These laws state that when an Emperor dies he becomes a god. However, a god cannot be an Emperor. The Emperor must be mortal: he must govern the country, fearing the wrath of Heaven. But what would a god be afraid of? What assurance could there be that he would govern justly? This could lead to general discontent and anarchy. The religious laws have been violated! The end is in sight for China!"

With a heavy heart the Emperor looked around at his courtiers.

"Very well!" he said. "If the country really is faced with such disaster, there is nothing for it. Bury me. I cannot wish for the end of China."

"It was ill-advised to have undertaken this trip, O Joy of the Universe! I always said it would bring misfortune upon you!" said Zhuar Fucian as he threw in the first shovelful of earth.

Deeply impressed by Zhuar Fucian's perspicacity, San Yanki's successor kept him on as Prime Minister and granted him even more powers.

To start, Zhuar Fucian had the Court Historian, First Master of Ceremonies and Chief Priest beheaded. As he said himself, they were all far too wily for their own good.

Translated by John Dewey

Rain

The Son of Heaven, Emperor Li O-a (may his name live longer than the universe!) was standing in the window of his porcelain palace. He was young and therefore still kind. Amidst the luxury and sparkle, he could not stop thinking about the poor and miserable.

It was raining torrentially. The sky was crying and its tears poured from trees and flowers. Sadness gripped the Emperor's heart and he exclaimed, "How miserable it is for the ones who, in this rain, do not have even a hat!" Turning to his Chamberlain, he said, "I would like to know how many such unfortunates there are in my Peking."

"Son of the Sun!" answered Tsung Hi-tsang, falling on his knees, "Is there anything impossible for the King of Kings? Before the sun goes down, O Father of Dawn, you will know what you wish to know."

The Emperor smiled graciously, and Tsung Hi-tsang

ran as fast as he could to the Prime Minister, San Chi-san. He ran in gasping for breath and, in his haste, he forgot even to honor the Prime Minister with all the salutations due his rank. Panting, he could hardly get out the words: "The Joy of the Universe, our most Gracious Sovereign, is terribly upset. He is upset by all the people who walk about without hats in the rain. He wants to know today how many there are of these people in Peking."

"Oh, there are such good-for-nothings in Peking," said San Chi-san. "Anyway..." And the Prime Minister summoned before him the mandarin Pi Hi-vo, Commander of the City.

"There are bad tidings from the palace," said San Chi-san as Pi Hi-vo, as was required, touched his forehead to the ground. "An impropriety has come to the attention of the Master of our Lives."

"How is that possible?" Pi Hi-vo cried in horror. "What has become of the magnificent garden with cool shadows that separates the palace from Peking?"

"I do not know exactly," said San Chi-san, but His Majesty is terribly upset by the scoundrels who walk about without hats in the rain. He wishes to know this very day how many such people there are in Peking. Find out!"

A minute later Pi Hi-vo shouted to his underlings, "Bring me this instant that old dog, Houar Dzung!" When the Commander of the City Guards, white with terror and trembling, fell at the feet of the mandarin, the latter covered him with curses. "Rascal! Good-for-nothing! Abominable traitor! Do you want us all to be sawn in half?"

"Please explain the reason for your ire," said Houar Dzung, shaking at the feet of the mandarin, "so that I may know how to console you. I am afraid I cannot understand the language of your wisdom."

"You are an old dog better fit to guard a herd of pigs than the greatest city in the world! The Emperor of China himself has noticed the improprieties that exist in your city, the scoundrels who do not have the decency even to wear a hat when gadding about in the rain. By evening I must know how many there are of them in Peking!"

"Everything will be done according to your wish." A second after banging his forehead on the floor three times at the feet of the mandarin, Houar Dzung was racing away to his guardsmen, called together by a deafening gong. "You rascals! I shall hang half of you so that the other half may be fried on red-hot coals. In what manner do you watch over the city? You permit people to walk about in the rain without hats on their heads! I give you one hour in which to seize every person without some kind of a hat on his head, even one made of straw!"

The guardsmen rushed off to carry out this order, and for the next hour Peking was the site of a massive manhunt. "Grab him! Seize him!" they cried, falling on the hatless far and wide. The offenders were dragged from behind fences and from inside houses where they tried to hide like rabbits wary of the cook who wants to turn them into a stew.

One minute before the hour was up, every hatless person in Peking was standing in the prison yard. "How many are there?" asked Houar Dzung.

"Twenty thousand eight hundred and seventy-one," said the guardsmen, bowing.

"Summon the executioners!" said Houar Dzung. Half an hour later, 20,871 headless Chinese were sprawled in the prison yard.

"The heads of 20,871 hatless scoundrels have been put on lances and carried through the streets as a lesson to the people of Peking," said Houar Dzung to Commander Pi

Hi-vo, who reported this to Prime Minister San Chi-san, who informed the Chamberlain Tsung-Hi-tsang.

Evening came. The rain stopped. A wandering wind dandled the trees, and a diamond rain flew from the trees to the sweet-smelling flowers, iridescent and afire from the rays of the setting sun. The whole garden was fragrant and aglitter as the Son of Heaven, Li O-a, stood in the window of his porcelain palace admiring the magnificent view. But being young and kind, even in this moment of aesthetic rapture, he did not forget the unfortunates.

"Oh, yes," he said, turning to Tsung Hi-tsang. "I did want to know how many people there are in Peking without a hat to cover their head in the rain."

"The Ruler of the Universe's wish has been fulfilled by his faithful servants," said Tsung Hi-tsang, bowing low.

"How many are there then? Tell me the truth," said the Emperor.

"In all Peking there is not one Chinese who does not have a hat to put on his head in the rain," said Tsung Hi-tsang. "I swear to you that that is the honest truth." Tsung Hi-tsang raised his hands and bowed his head in the sign of a sacred oath.

The face of the kind Emperor lit up with a happy and joyful smile. "Happy city! Happy nation!" he beamed. "And how happy am I in the knowledge that under my rule the people are so prosperous."

Everyone in the palace was happy upon seeing the happiness of the Emperor.

San Chi-san, Pi Hi-vo, and Houar Dzung all received the Order of the Golden Dragon for their fatherly care of the people.

Translated by Rowen Glie

Rewards

People do like to make a lot of noise at court, despite the fact that protocol decrees complete silence. The following incident took place at one time in Peking.

The Emperor Yuan Hozan woke late one morning in a bad mood. Summoning his Chief Eunuch, he said: "I have slept too late to hear the reports of my councilors and to issue decrees concerning the government of the country. What is more, I have missed morning prayers, so that now the souls of my ancestors will be displeased and angered and will no doubt visit misfortunes upon China and myself. And all this disorder in Heaven and on earth has come about because there was an animal prowling the palace grounds last night, making noise under my window and keeping me awake."

"I wonder if a tiger could have got into the grounds?" said the Chief Eunuch, trembling all over.

The Emperor merely shrugged: "You always dream up bugbears and demons where none exist. This was no tiger: the noise it made was much quieter."

"Then perhaps it was a donkey?" exclaimed the Chief Eunuch. "Donkeys too make a most disagreeable noise!"

"No," remarked the Emperor after some thought, "it was not the noise a donkey makes. I know what a donkey sounds like. This was much, much quieter. The creature made a noise like this… I took note."

And the Emperor demonstrated the sound made by the mysterious creature.

"Very well," said the Chief Eunuch. "I shall summon all our scholars to the palace immediately. Let them draw upon the sum total of their learning, let them search through all books ancient and modern and resolve what manner of creature it was!"

With these words he departed, bowing innumerable times, then calmly returned to his quarters, where he drank tea and lay on his bed. Some three hours later he appeared before the Emperor once more. "Proving themselves equal to their calling, the scholars have solved the riddle," he announced. "That creature which kept you from your sleep, O Son of Heaven, is known to our scholars under the name of 'frog', and is one of the most cunning creatures upon earth. It lives in the grass and, to avoid capture, has deliberately affected tiny proportions, extreme speed, and green coloring!"

"Indeed! Under these circumstances it will be very difficult to catch the creature in the grass," said the Emperor. "Nevertheless it is my earnest wish that you should attempt to do so. Catch it, destroy it, in effect, do whatever is necessary so that I may sleep, pray and conduct the affairs of state."

"As you can see, O Son of Heaven, the fulfillment of your wish is well-nigh impossible!" exclaimed the Chief Eunuch. "Nevertheless we shall make every effort, drawing upon all the resources of energy and intellect at our disposal, and our love and devotion to Your Highness will perhaps enable us to accomplish this task with honor!"

"I thank you in anticipation of that!" said the Emperor, touched by these words. "Let it be known to all that I shall make it my business to reward the diligence of each and every one."

Bowing the requisite number of times, the Chief Eunuch took his leave and told the lowest-ranking eunuch: "There is a frog on the palace grounds. Give the command for it to be caught and destroyed!"

The lowest-ranking eunuch passed the command on

to the palace Majordomo, who passed it on to the Head Gardener, who passed it on to the Superintendant of Roses, who passed it on to the Head Waterer. The Head Waterer summoned the laborer Tun Li and told him: "Go and catch a frog!"

Tun Li went out into the palace grounds, caught a frog that was hopping along one of the paths and, holding it by its hind legs, hit its head against a stone. Then he took the frog to the Head Waterer and laid it at his feet. "There you are, sir," he said.

The Head Waterer took the frog to the Superintendant of Roses, who took it to the Head Gardener, who took it to the Majordomo, who took it to the lowest-ranking eunuch, who took it to the Chief Eunuch and announced: "Here is the frog, caught and destroyed."

"Goodness gracious, no!" said the Chief Eunuch. "That would be far too straightforward!" And he had the largest gong sounded to summon all the palace retinue: huntsmen, guards, soldiers, eunuchs and priests.

A fearful tumult arose.

Looking out of his window, the Emperor saw the Master Huntsman go past and marveled at his weapons. Clad in armor, the Master Huntsman had as many as ten daggers bristling from his belt. He was wearing two swords, one at his right side and the other at his left, in case the first one broke. In one hand he held a spear with red feathers, and in the other a bow fashioned from ebony, its string stretched fearsomely taut. Over his shoulders were slung two quivers filled with arrows. On one of the quivers was written in bold characters: `Do not touch! Poisoned arrows!' and on the other: `May be touched. Non-poisoned arrows.'

He was followed by the other huntsmen marching in ranks, who proceeded to cordon off the grounds of the palace. There was a huntsman standing with his bow drawn behind every bush.

The guards occupied the palace, taking up positions with weapons drawn by every door and window in case the creature, startled by the hue and cry, should take it into its head to dart into the palace. As a further precaution, a detachment of soldiers was drawn up in battle formation in the courtyard.

In the temple the priests offered up prayers to the gods for a successful outcome to the hunt.

The eunuchs comforted the Emperor's tearful wives in the inner chambers and told them stories.

In the midst of all this tumult the Emperor paced up and down, encouraging the various groups of retainers with promises of rewards to come.

So passed the whole day.

And when night fell upon the earth, engulfing the flowers in the palace gardens in darkness so that only the fragrance told of their presence, the air was suddenly rent by a thunderous cry of victory.

The Chief Eunuch came running in to the Emperor, prostrated himself before him and exclaimed: "The frog has been slain!"

After him came six eunuchs bearing a massive gold platter on which lay a little green frog with a white belly and its head smashed in.

"Most remarkable!" cried the Emperor. "How on earth could they see such a tiny creature in the dark?"

"All thanks to diligent effort," replied the Chief Eunuch, bowing low before the Emperor. "As you can see, it was no easy task," he continued with a sigh. "Of course, I had overall responsibility for bringing all these people together and deploying them to their various tasks. Even so I cannot take all of the credit for this glorious frog hunt. Every single person worked conscientiously — the entire palace staff without exception."

The Emperor frowned. "No, not everyone!" he remarked. "This afternoon, as I was going around the palace gardens and various outbuildings to inspect my huntsmen, guards and soldiers, I observed one idle fellow dressed in the clothes of a simple laborer. While everyone else was engaged in hunting the creature, this fellow was lying on his stomach, warming his back in the sun. Find out his name!"

The Chief Eunuch ran off to do the Emperor's bidding.

The man in question was none other than Tun Li. After catching the frog and delivering it to the Head Waterer, he had lain down in the sun and remained in that attitude for the rest of the day.

He was soon identified, and the Chief Eunuch hurried back to the Emperor to report: "The idler's name is Tun Li!"

"How could he just lie there like a pig wallowing in mud while everyone else was working so hard to catch the frog?" exclaimed the angry Emperor.

"Because idleness and indolence are second nature to him!" the Chief Eunuch shrugged. "One can't expect more from these simple folk. What do they care about anything? Habitual layabouts and dawdlers, who like nothing better than a good lie-down! Anything they do they turn into an excuse for a holiday."

"Very well!" exclaimed the Emperor. "I shall know how to reward each in accordance with his merits."

And he scattered favors about him with a generous hand. The Chief Eunuch was awarded the governorship of the richest province for three years, together with all its revenues.

The other eunuchs each received a golden robe for comforting the Emperor's wives during the crisis.

The priests were showered with money for the efficacy of their prayers, and more sacrificial victims were placed at their disposal than they normally received in the course of a whole year.

The Master Huntsman had all his weapons set with precious stones.

All the other huntsmen received gifts of expensive weaponry, as did the guards who had protected the palace during the hunt.

Even the scholars, quite unexpectedly for them, were rewarded, some receiving additional tassels for their hats, others the Tunic of Merit, and others still the title of Mandarin.

As for Tun Li, he was ordered to be given fifty strokes on the soles of his feet with bamboo sticks 'for his sloth, idleness and inactivity during the hunt for the frog'. This punishment, which he received lying down, was administered by the Head Gardener with the Chief Eunuch looking on and counting the strokes.

Strange indeed are the ways of the world.

"Often the one who is lying down should be standing, while the one who is standing should be lying down," as the Chinese proverb has it.

Translated by John Dewey

Not the Right Heels

As with everything in China, this tale is very deep, full of wisdom, and highly instructive.

Men are like guns: they are loaded from the rear! Teachers tell us that it is people's heads that must be loaded, and with good ideas. But rulers everywhere load them with good ideas from the rear, starting from the back and lower down. The Chinese, in case you didn't know, take this to the limit: they suggest correct ideas to their citizens with bamboo canes applied to the heels. Why the heels? Probably because the fear of punishment, as everyone knows, makes the soul of a man sink to his heels. Thus, the heels become the right place, the address, to which to send, by means of bamboo canes, the best suggestions and ideas.

The Son of the Sun, Brother of the Moon, Father of all Stars in the Sky, the Conqueror of all Nations on Earth, Ruler of all Kings, Emperors, Sultans, and Knights, the Great, Mighty, and Wisest Emperor of China, Ching Chang, was presiding over a meeting of the government council surrounded by his most noble mandarins. The Emperor became pensive and, his voice sounding like bells, said, "In our wisdom we would like to know what happens in our China. Among you, my chosen mandarins, we see our good Tun Li. He is the head of our police. He is in charge of our food supply and our good morals. He feeds the people with rice and bamboo. The glorious and wise Tun Li, arise! And without fear for your noble heels, tell us how things are in China."

In a sign of respect for the Emperor, everyone raised their fingers. Tun Li rose and said, after the traditional 472 bows, "Son of Heaven! A dog will bark at the moon. This gives me the courage to speak in your presence. The worthless worm will tell the truth, because a lie must be invented. But, where will the brainless worm find the brains to do that? Only clever men can invent; for a nitwit, the truth is good enough. Nanking fights Canton, Peking makes war with Nanking, Canton fights Shanghai. And still, China is blooming. The blooming of our great China is such that foreign devils are green with envy. It is enough for me to tell you one thing, O Greatest and Wisest of Emperors: the prosperity of China today is such that our hens have begun laying golden eggs."

"What? Golden eggs?" cried the Emperor. And his voice had the sound of silver bells. "But this can happen only in fairytales!"

After making the ritual 372 bows, Tun Li said, "It happens also in a country of fabulous prosperity, in China. Were you not the Emperor of China, I would say, 'Without stepping on the insignificant worm who talks to you, take a walk to the market and look around by yourself.' What is the cost of ten eggs? Ten golden coins! Every egg is a golden coin! In other countries a man must work from dawn to dusk to earn a golden coin. And in China? A hen cackles and lays a golden coin! Cackle, cackle, and a golden coin!"

The mandarins all raised their finger to signify their amazement, but the sage, Chi San, said, "Where chickens enjoy life, men live in sadness."

The Emperor looked at him with benevolence, made a sign to him to be silent, and said, "Our great teacher, Chi San, is very wise. Therefore, you, Tun Li, pay no attention to him. For what is the purpose of wisdom if not to cloud our joys? Clouds are in the sky to hide the sun. How did you put it, Tun Li? Cackle, cackle, and a golden coin? Yes! Cackle, cackle, and a golden coin! Cackle, cackle, and a golden coin! Cackle, cackle, and a golden coin!"

The government council, ecstatic, began repeating, "Cackle, cackle, and a golden coin!" Never had they had such an enjoyable conference.

The Emperor ordered the gong to be rung, and said, "I declare this meeting of the government council closed. The government council is a place of boredom, worry, and sadness. I am too happy, too glad, and too joyful in my soul to sit in this gloomy place! On the occasion of this happy event, I hereby declare a three day holiday in Peking, with popular amusements, fireworks, and illuminations."

The members of the council left the meeting joyfully repeating, "Cackle, cackle, and a golden coin! Cackle, cackle, and a golden coin!"

In a joyful mood, Emperor Ching Chang strolled out into his garden. The first mandarin of the lowest class that he met, he raised to the rank of first class. Thus, his eldest son's wet nurse was suddenly made a general and marshal. He continued his stroll, distributing right and left Orders of the Dragon, colored jackets, and buttons for people's hats like stars in the Milky Way.

He soon came to a secluded hut where, among the flowers, lived the sage Chi San. "I like sages only from afar," said the Emperor. "Coming closer, there is nothing to talk with them about. You wise men will not be satisfied with a reward of the Order of the Dragon of the third, second, or even the first degree. Yellow or blue jackets do not make you happy. Even to have buttons on your hats is of no interest to you."

"O Great and Glorious Emperor," said the sage, "if you, in your limitless benevolence, would make me a gift of a dozen eggs, I would not be able to find words enough in our Chinese language to thank you."

"What! You? A sage?" cried the Emperor in surprise. "You would be happy to receive such a paltry gift?"

"Do you think that only nitwits must eat?" asked Chi San. "I have had the honor to report to you that where life is good for chickens, it is very hard for people. It is very nice to say, 'Cackle, cackle, and a golden coin!' But at the present cost of eggs, people must die from hunger."

"Let the dragon have that cursed Tun Li," cried the Emperor. "He made a rooster out of me, Son of Heaven, ruler over 500 million Chinese. He rejoiced as if I were a rooster in a hen house! Cackle, cackle, and a golden coin!" The Emperor so lost his good humor that he forgot to order a dozen eggs for the sage. He hurried to the palace and put an immediate stop to all the festivities, amusements, fireworks, and illuminations. Then he called an emergency meeting of the government council in order to discuss very important business.

The government council convened immediately. The great Emperor was somber and his voice was like the roar of a war drum. "Contemptible Tun Li," said the Emperor, "today you described China as flourishing but I have found out that our nation is ruined. Our hens lay eggs which cost a golden coin each, and the sage Chi San, the pride, the ornament, and glory of our reign, must, because of this, die from starvation. Think what our descendants, the chroniclers, and the history books will say: 'Ching Chang – during the reign of this Emperor, the renown, wise, and great sage Chi San, the grace and ornament of the Heavenly Empire, died of hunger.' An eight-year-old boy will be asked in school, 'For what is the Emperor Ching Chang remembered?' and the little imp will answer, 'In the reign of Ching Chang sages starved. In his reign the greatest philosopher of China, Chi San, died of hunger.' And the teacher, instead of giving him the rod, will say, 'Good boy!' My name will be crossed out by my descendants from their list of ancestors. My name will be a derision and shame for all future generations of China. This is what you brought me, you contemptible Tun Li, with your bragging: Cackle, cackle, and a golden coin!"

Tun Li had to protect his heels. He leapt out of his seat, made the ritual 637 bows, and said, "Great Emperor! If you will permit the stupid son of my father to speak, I would like to say a word."

"Our mercy is limitless," replied the Emperor. "We allow you to make the air stink once more with your breath. We will listen to what the most insignificant of all our worms has to say."

"Son of Heaven!" said Tun Li, kissing the Emperor's feet, "the nature of the crime has been determined. Eggs cost a golden coin each. Now we must determine whose are the guilty heels." And all the mandarins agreed that the words of Tun Li were in strict accordance with the law and the customs of the Heavenly Empire.

"Only be careful to find the right heels," warned the sage Chi San.

"Exactly!" Tun Li happily agreed. "Wisdom speaks with thy mouth, great and wise Chi San! Exactly! The right heels. And whose heels are to blame for the high price of eggs? Who in the villages sell eggs? Who resells them to the city? The peasants! Their heels are at the bottom of all this. Order enough strokes with bamboo canes on their heels and the price of eggs will go down!"

Whereupon the Emperor said, "Your advice, I think, is dictated by wisdom itself. Give the order, Tun Li."

Tun Li gave the order. Seven bamboo groves were cut down in an effort to suggest to the peasants the right price for eggs. But the price of eggs went up. Now they were sold in the market for two golden coins each. The peasants now wanted twice as much for their eggs. "One golden coin for each egg and one for the bamboo strokes," they said. "Do you think that our heels are worth nothing?"

For a long time the Emperor did not see his very wise teacher. The sage Chi San was bedridden in his hut, dying from hunger, among his flowers. The Emperor came to see him. "Such a proven remedy as bamboo, and even this did not help!" cried the Emperor in deep distress.

And the sage, gathering his last strength, murmured, "The wrong heels, Son of Heaven!"

The Emperor reconvened the government council in order to consult. "Frankly speaking," said the Emperor, and his words were like cold tea, "I do not like sages. They are troublesome people, so different from ordinary people who live while life is in them and then, when death comes, die quietly and meekly – a pleasure to watch. Oh, God, please be responsibility before posterity. Died? Why? What for? How did it all happen? The great Chi San is at death's door again. Eggs cost more than before. Never was immortality closer to Chi San than it is now. All your efforts, Tun Li, were for naught."

"O Son of Heaven. Do not spoil with sorrow your divine liver. Your liver is needed by China," cried Tun Li after making the requisite 837 bows. "The evil is known: the high price of eggs. The remedy was found: bamboo! The mistake was in its application. The bamboo was applied to the wrong heels."

"Right! Right! Even the wise Chi San says, 'The wrong heels'!" replied the Emperor.

"I, the stupid son of my father, am happy to be of the same opinion as that of our great sage," continued Tun Li. "This means that we need not only apply the bamboo to the heels of the peasants. Remember that any sale involves two people: the one who sells at the high price and the one who buys at the high price. Why do residents of Peking pay two golden coins for one egg? In so doing, they concur with the high price, spread greediness, and spoil the peasants. The buyers should receive bamboo strokes on their heels. They should not spread vice. It is as necessary to fight the greedy as it is to fight the profligate."

"Tun Li!" exclaimed the Emperor, "Your reasoning is

constructed according to all the laws of logic and justice! Tun Li, give the order!"

"This time it will be necessary to use many bamboo canes," said the mandarin in charge of the state treasury.

"Would I begrudge my subjects bamboo?" asked the Emperor with compassion.

And the fight against the money squanderers spread to all the markets of Peking.

The fight lasted three days – three long days. On the fourth day the cost of an egg reached four golden coins. No one was brave enough to buy eggs openly. Eggs were now sold only on the black market, so the price doubled.

The very wise Chi San, being very intelligent, did not go to the market himself, but sent his housekeeper. The woman returned from the market on her tiptoes, like a ballerina; she could not walk on her heels. And instead of four eggs, she brought only one.

The Emperor, in his limitless wisdom, decided to visit Chi San and inquire about his health. He found Chi San close to death. The sage pointed to his heels, and murmured, "The wrong ones…"

The Emperor started to cry: "Chi San! Wise One! Great One! My teacher! Wait! Do not die just yet. I swear to you by all the dragons that tomorrow everything will be fixed. I shall chop off the head of Tun Li, that good-for-nothing."

The Emperor again convened the government council.

The government council came to order. The Son of Heaven was irate. Lightning was in his eyes. His voice was like thunder when he exclaimed, "You good-for-nothing, Tun Li! Prepare to put on the execution block the rotten onion which you dare to call your head. The great Chi San is dying and history is preparing to cover our names with shame."

Tun Li fell at the feet of the Emperor and exclaimed, "What difference will it make if you cut off such rubbish as my head today or tomorrow? One day of life, O Master of the Universe, and I swear to you that the right heels will be found. We looked over all the heels in China but we did not find the truly guilty ones. I have now found the right heels. Who lays eggs? Hens! Hens should receive bamboo strokes on their heels. Do not lay expensive eggs! Do not! Do not!" The government council began to beam with joy, listening to this simple, clear, and obvious solution.

"Tun Li, give the order!" the Emperor commanded him. And Tun Li gave the order.

All day long it was impossible anywhere in China to hear oneself think, so loud was the cackling of hens. The hens were caught, turned upside down, and beaten on their tiny heels.

The next day the hens stopped laying eggs.

In mortal fear, the Emperor went to visit the wise Chi San in his house among the flowers. Chi San, with a gentle smile, gathered his last strength, and said to the Emperor, who was crying at his feet, "You are interested, Son of Heaven, in what the history books will say about you? Do not worry; they will not say anything bad. History will say, 'Ching Chang was a good Emperor. He meant well. He had only one misfortune; he never could find the right heels.' But do not worry, Son of Heaven. This is the fate of many, many Emperors on this earth. They always punish the wrong heels."

So said the wise Chi San as he died.

Translated by Rowen Glie

Conscience

This happened many eons ago, before history was written down. Even then, people did foolish things, but no one wrote them down. This must be why we consider our ancestors truly wise men.

It was in that time out of mind that Conscience was born. She was born one silent night when everything was thinking. The river was deep in thought and glittering in the moonshine, the reeds along its banks were still, and the grasses and the skies were also lost in thought. Thinking is the reason why, at night, everything is so silent. During the day, the world is full of noise and everyone is busy with living, doing all sorts of things; but at night, everything is silent and engaged in thinking. Every chrysalis thinks about the bright stripes with which it should let the butterfly out. At night the plants invent flowers, the nightingales their songs, and the stars the future.

On just such a night, when everything was thinking, Conscience was born. She was born with eyes as big as those of night birds. The moonlight painted her face pale, and stars lit fire in the depth of her eyes. And Conscience went to live on the earth.

Her life was half good and half bad. Like an owl, she was lived by night. During the day, no one wanted to talk to her: too busy! Here they build, there they dig. She would approach someone and he would push her aside, saying, "Don't you see what's going on around you? Here they carry stones, here they drag logs, and here the horse-drawn carts are at work. Here you must watch out not to be run over. Is this any time to talk?"

However, at night she could walk at her leisure. She

would visit the houses of the rich made of porcelain or the bamboo huts of the poor. She would touch the sleeping man's shoulder. He would wake and see in the darkness her fiery eyes, and he would ask, "What do you want?"

"What did you do today?" Conscience would ask.

"What did I do? Nothing!"

"Think it over! ... Think again!"

"Well, maybe..."

Then Conscience would leave him and go to the next man, but the first man would be unable to sleep and toss and turn till morning, all the time thinking over the wrongs he had done that day. Many wrong acts which he had been unable to recognize as such during the day would become obvious to him at night.

There were only a very few people now who were able to sleep. Everyone suffered from sleeplessness. Even the rich could not be helped by doctors, not even opium worked. Li Chan Dzu, the wise one, knew of no remedy for sleepless nights. He had more money, more property, and more land than anybody. "Since he has more of everything than anybody else," people thought, "he must also have more brains than anybody else." They called Li Chan Dzu "The Wisest".

But even the wisest Li Chan Dzu, who suffered more than anyone from this sickness, did not know what to do. All the people were in his debt, and passed their lives in working out their debts to him. This was how the wise Li Chan Dzu organized things. As a wise man he always knew what to do. When someone who owed him money stole something from him and was caught, Li Chan Dzu would beat him and, in his wisdom, would do it in such a way as to make an example of him to others. During the day, this procedure would seem very wise because the others would become, at least for a short while, too fearful to steal. But, at night, other ideas would come into Li Chan Dzu's head: "Why is he stealing? Because he has nothing to eat. He cannot make a living. He has to work for me for nothing, just to pay off his debt to me." And the wise Li Chan Dzu would even laugh: "What do you know! It is they who steal, and now I am the one who is in the wrong." He could laugh, but he could not sleep.

In the end, he could not abide his sleepless nights. In spite of all his wisdom, he made a decision, and he said, "I will give them back all their money, all their properties, and all their houses."

Now the relatives of the wise Li Chan Dzu raised a hue and cry. "It is his insomnia that makes him so foolish," they declared. "Because of sleepless nights, foolishness overcame this wise man." The doctors agreed.

A general vituperation arose. "Conscience is guilty of all that. If foolishness can overcome the wisest of men, what will happen to us, who are not so wise?" Everyone became frightened. Everyone complained, "I, too, have lost sleep." "And so have I…" "And so have I…"

The poor were frightened even more than the rich. "We have less of everything therefore we have less wisdom too. What then will happen to our poor little brains?"

And the rich said, "Do you see how Conscience frightens the poor? Who will defend them?"

With that, everyone started to think how to get rid of Conscience. But no matter how many wise people they consulted no one could think of a solution.

At this time there lived in Nanking a man by the name of A Pu O. He was so wise and so learned that he had no equal in all of China. People said, "We shall seek out his advice. He is the only one who can help us." They sent messengers, brought gifts, bowed many times down to the ground, and pleaded, "Deliver us from the sleeplessness inflicted by Conscience!"

A Pu O listened to the people's pleadings, reflected, smiled, and said, "I can help you. I can make it so that Conscience will not have the right to enter your houses."

Everyone pricked up their ears! A Pu O smiled again, and said, "Let us create laws so that the ignorant man will know what is permitted and what is not. Let us then write on scrolls what a man should do and what he should not. The mandarins will learn the laws by heart, and everyone else will come to them to ask what is and what is not permitted. Then, let Conscience come and ask, 'What did you do today?' And the people will answer, 'I did what is written on the scrolls.' And everyone will sleep peacefully. Of course the mandarins will be paid, for it shall not be for nothing that they will fill their brains with the laws.

Every one was happy: the mandarins, because it is easier to learn laws than to hoe the earth; and the others, because it is better to pay the mandarins for a few minutes of their time by day than to talk to Conscience by night.

So they started to write down laws about what men should and should not do. Finally they had it all in writing.

The wise A Pu O was made the Supreme Mandarin. People returned to their everyday lives and their faces even became fuller. If a man had to do something he would go immediately to the mandarin and lay his gifts before him. If there was a disagreement between two people, both would go to the mandarin with gifts. "Take out your scrolls," they would say, "and tell us what to do." Only the very poorest people, with nothing to bring to the mandarin, continued to suffer from sleeplessness. Everyone else, when Conscience came to see them at night, would say, "I acted according to the law! To the scrolls! I did nothing by myself." And they would turn over and fall back to sleep.

Even the wise Li Chan Dzu, who suffered most from sleepless nights, would only smile at Conscience and say, "Hello, my beautiful one, how are you?"

"What about the land and the money you wanted to return?" Conscience would ask, looking at him with eyes that shone like stars.

"But do I have the right to do that?" Li Chan Dzu would ask laughingly. "What does it say in the scrolls? 'The property of each person belongs to him and his heirs.' How can I give up property that belongs not only to me, if my heirs will not consent? If I were to do that, I would be a thief stealing from my own heirs, or a lunatic stealing from myself. The law says that 'A thief or a lunatic must be put on a chain.' So leave me in peace and let me sleep quietly. And I suggest that you also go to sleep and not roam the streets at night." With that, Li Chan Dzu would turn over and fall fast asleep.

Wherever Conscience went she heard the same story: "What do we know? We do what the mandarins say. Do not ask us! Ask them. We obey the law." Thus it was that Conscience went to the mandarins.

"Why is it that no one wants to listen to me?" Conscience asked.

The mandarins laughed. "What are laws for? How can we allow people to listen to you and act accordingly? What if they should misunderstand you and get all mixed up? But here are our laws, written for everyone, with India ink on yellow paper. And a marvelous thing they are! No wonder A Pu O was made the Supreme Mandarin."

Conscience now went to A Pu O himself. While he slept, she touched his shoulder and stood aside. A-Pu-O awoke and leapt out of his bed. "How dare you to come into someone else's house without an invitation! What does the law say? 'He who comes stealthily into another man's house shall be considered a thief and put in prison.'"

"I did not come to steal from you; I am Conscience!"

"According to law, you are a depraved woman," replied A Pu O. "It is clearly stated, 'If a woman comes at night to visit a man who is not her husband, she is considered a depraved woman and must be put in prison.' You are a whore, if not a thief."

"I am a whore?" cried Conscience, "How dare you!"

"If you are not a whore or a thief," said A Pu O, "you simply do not wish to obey the law. We have a law for this too: 'Whoever will not obey the law shall be considered a desperado and put into prison.' Hey! Men! Put this woman in chains and behind bars as a whore, and a suspected thief, caught obstructing the law." Thus, Conscience was put in chains and behind bars.

Since then Conscience has not visited anyone, or made trouble for anyone; she has been all but forgotten. Only now and then, some ruffian who is mad at a mandarin will cry, "You have no Conscience!"

Then immediately a paper will be shown to him to prove that Conscience exists, but it is kept under lock and key: "We have a Conscience, but we keep her locked up."

And the ruffian will fall silent, thinking, "They are right. They do have a Conscience."

Ever since then people have lived quietly and well.

Translated by Rowen Glie

The Good Emperor

The Emperor Fan Djin Dsan — whom the historians call Mun-Su or "Father of the People" — was a good emperor who took good care of his subjects. When rumors reached him that one of the viceroys was vexing his subjects, he would summon the troublesome viceroy together with the executioner, and say to the executioner, "Off with his head! I hope that in the next world, they will recognize him even without his head, just by his wrongdoings." He would then replace the late viceroy with another, recommended to him by his councilors and ministers.

He always read the reports of the viceroys himself. In their reports, the viceroys said that China was enjoying an unparalleled period of prosperity, that the sun shone with amazing accuracy, that the rains came in the right season, and that the peasants did not know what to do with all their extra rice. The Emperor read all this and thought, "And what if it is a lie?" Then an idea came to him. On an appointed day he summoned all his councilors, ministers, and the courtiers to the palace. Seated on his throne, he declared, "My viceroys report that China is enjoying an unparalleled period of prosperity, that the Chinese do not know what to do with all their extra rice. Bearing in mind the good of our people, we have decided to think about this, to pray to the gods and consult the ancestors, 'What should we do with all the extra rice so that it would be for the good of the people?' From now on, we will go into seclusion in the private rooms of our palace and we will keep ourselves busy with prayers, reflections, and spiritual talks with the ancestors. And since, thank the gods, we have many ancestors, we suppose that it will take at least three moons before we finish our talks with them, without offending any of them by omission. Therefore, during these three moons, we forbid anyone to come to the palace or to trouble us with problems. For three moons we will be invisible to all except Heaven."

The ministers, the councilors, and the courtiers praised the wisdom of the Emperor and happily went home.

In the meantime, the Emperor called for a few of his most loyal servants, changed his imperial robes for the rags of a beggar, made his servants do the same, and in secret left the palace and went to travel through China to find out if the reports of the viceroys reflected the reality in China, if the people were really prospering, and if they were really delighted with their rulers.

The first province on the Emperor's route was the province of Pe Chi Li. Arriving there, the Emperor and his companions came to a house and begged, "In the name of your ancestors, whose virtues beautified the earth and now adorn the Heaven, give a handful of rice to unfortunates dying from hunger."

In reply they heard, "Because you are beggars, you must be from our province and subject to our viceroy. However, because you ask us to give you something, you must come from a very distant part of China. Therefore, go away, poor man."

The Emperor and his companions came to another house. In answer to their plea for a handful of rice, they were told, "It is no good to laugh at another man's misfortunes."

At the third house, the people just started to weep upon hearing their plea for a handful of rice.

In the fourth house, the master of the house raised his head and asked, "Rice? Who is it: a mandarin or an animal?"

The Emperor smiled and said, "The viceroy of Pe Chi Li wrote the truth. Truly, if someone would give rice to these people, they would not know what to do with it. They appear never to have seen rice before in their life."

In the morning the Emperor set about visiting temples in an attempt to overhear what the people were praying for. The stomachs of the Chinese were empty, but the temples were full. In all the temples there were crowds of people all repeating the same prayer: "Holy ancestors, beg Heaven to inspire our good, solicitous Emperor, Fan Djin Dsan, with the excellent idea of cutting off the head of our viceroy, Tun Fa O. The world has never known such a terrible cheat and robber."

Thus it was that all the people prayed in all the temples. One day, however, the Emperor arrived very early in the morning and found an old man praying with a particular fervor. Everyone prayed with fervor but this old man prayed with greater fervor than anyone else. In order to hear what the old man was praying for, the Emperor came closer and heard, "Holy ancestors, inspire our good but restless Emperor Fan Djin Dsan to allow Tun Fa-O to be our viceroy for many years to come. And let Heaven permit Tun Fa O to live to a very old age and then start to live again."

The Emperor was amazed. When the old man ended his devotion, the Emperor asked him, "Tell me, venerated father, has Tun Fa O been particularly good to you? Is that why you pray for him?"

The old man grinned. "The mother of the mother of the man for whom Tun Fa O has done anything good has not yet been born. One can see that you are a stranger here. Otherwise, you would not ask such stupid questions."

"But maybe you like Tun Fa O for his appearance, his lordly carriage. Have you ever seen him in the flesh?" asked the Emperor.

Before answering, the old man said a short prayer to

his ancestors. "Thank the gods, I have never, ever in my life laid eyes on him, nor has he laid eyes on me."

The Emperor was now completely astonished. "Why, then, are you praying for him when everyone else in this province prays for just one thing: that the Emperor cut off the head of Tun Fa O as soon as possible?"

"Why?" asked the old one. "Because they are young and stupid, and do not know the world. I have survived three viceroys. We had Zu Li Ku as our viceroy and he was a greedy man, a cruel man was he. Under him, the whole province moaned and we prayed to Heaven, from morning to evening, 'Let our Emperor cut off the head of Zu Li Ku!' Heaven listened to us and murmured this idea to the Emperor. The Emperor summoned Zu Li Ku to Peking and ordered his head cut off. Then they sent us the mandarin Kaang Chi Yu. Kaang Chi Yu happened to be even more rapacious and cruel. The province of Pe Chi Li now clamored even more loudly, imploring the gods to give our Emperor the idea of cutting off the head of Kaang Chi Yu. Again Heaven listened to us: the Emperor recalled Kaang Chi Yu and had his head cut off. Then they sent us the present Tun Fa O, let Heaven prolong his life by many long, long, years! You may cross the whole province in its length and width and you will not find here one happy face or one sated person. We plant tears instead of rice and what grows is grief. So the people, in their stupidity, implore Heaven to suggest to the Emperor the idea of cutting off Tun Fa O's head. And I, an old man, I am afraid that Heaven may listen to them. The Emperor will cut off the head of Tun Fa O and send us another viceroy. And what if the next viceroy is even worse than Tun Fa O? While I think that nothing can be worse than Tun Fa-O, how can one be sure of it? No, let this one remain, and let Heaven prolong his life by many, many years."

Listening to all this, the Emperor became very distressed. He did not even try to travel through other provinces. He returned straight away to Peking and went to the palace. He called his ministers and councilors, and all the courtiers, and he said, "Our council with our ancestors lasted less long than we expected – because our ancestors have been very brief in their advice. They all said, 'From now on, no matter what rumors reach us about our viceroys, they shall not be replaced.' And so be it!"

All praised the wisdom of the Emperor.

But more than anyone, the old man in the province of Pe Chi Li praised the very great wisdom of the Emperor.

Translated by Rowen Glie

Chinese Jurisprudence

The mandarin Qin Hozan was the wisest of judges. And since wise judges are a rarity in China, people even came from other provinces to have their cases heard by him.

However many bribes Qin Hozan may have accepted, it was not this that wore the old man down. What he really found tiresome was the same old story being played out again and again. Whenever a criminal case came up, the accused would throw himself at the judge's feet and launch into a vociferous lament:

"Qin Hozan, beware of impetuosity! My case is a civil one and has nothing to do with criminal law. By all means direct me to pay compensation to the plaintiff should your conscience dictate, but there is no reason to send me to jail. It's a question of money, a civil case. So judge me in accordance with civil, not criminal law."

If on the other hand he had a civil case to decide, both plaintiff and respondent would throw themselves at his feet. The plaintiff would cry:

"Qin Hozan, beware of compassion! What good is it to me if you order him to pay compensation? Send him to jail! This is no civil case. The scoundrel refuses to pay what he owes. That's plain fraud, a criminal offence!"

At the same time the respondent would lie weeping at the judge's feet: "Qin Hozan! Do you wish for once in your life to dispense justice? Send this monster to jail for demanding money from people who don't owe him anything! It's an open-and-shut case of fraud! Qin Hozan! What good will it do if you dismiss his claim in accordance with civil law? The villain belongs in jail! It's a criminal matter!"

This had been going on throughout Qin Hozan's life, and eventually he grew heartily sick of the whole business. As the Chinese proverb has it, by the ninth bowl even the tastiest soup has lost its flavor.

As he had two grown sons, both strapping young fellows, he called them to him and said: "You've spent too long letting the grass grow under your feet here in China. Here's some money: go to Europe. That's the name of a country where even the sun arrives late. Spend the money on studying. There knowledge is sold the way food is here: they try to foist you off with out-of-date goods. I've heard of two subjects in particular taught there, civil and criminal law. One of you will study civil law, the other criminal law. Then come back and tell me all you know, and at last I shall know the difference between the two. You may go."

His sons made preparations for the journey and with many tears set off for Europe. They were away for four years, moving from place to place and studying wherever they went.

Their father received letters from cities with the most extraordinary names: Pa-Ris, Lon-Don, Vien-Na, Ber-Lin. One was even headed: "Moulin-Rouge". Each letter ended with the words: "The barbarians are greedy, and knowledge is sweet, so send us more money."

In the end the old man grew tired of this. One day after receiving another of these letters he didn't send any money. And after thirty days and thirty nights his sons returned. They returned thin and emaciated, with sunken eyes, scarcely able to stand on their shaky legs.

"I should like to think that is the result of studying!" said Qin Hozan, and he commanded his sons: "Tell me everything you learnt in the course of your studies in that far-off land where even the sun arrives late. First of all, elder son, tell me what a civil case involves, and then you, younger son, can tell me about the criminal variety, so that I, old man that I am, shall know how to deal with cases brought by litigants."

The sons bowed and began their accounts.

First the elder son spent two hours outlining what in the eyes of legal experts constitutes a civil action.

Then for three hours the younger son gave a detailed exposition of what qualifies as a criminal action. The sun, already weary, was sinking toward the horizon. The old man was weary too.

'Have you finished at last?' he asked.

'We have.'

'Oh, oh, oh!'

Qin Hozan thought for a moment, smiled and said: "I see that the white barbarians do indeed sell knowledge as our tradesmen sell pork. They try to get as much money as they can for it and palm you off with rotten goods! They should be beaten on their heels with bamboo canes. Five hours you've spent on this nonsense, yet as far as I can see it's all quite simple. In a criminal case, only one scoundrel is visible, the person who stands accused in the dock. A civil case, on the other hand, can be defined as one in which it's difficult to see who the scoundrel is: the person filing the claim or the one he's filing it against. That's the only difference between a civil and a criminal trial. So in a criminal case the one person up before the court should be beaten on his heels with bamboo canes, whereas in a civil case both of them should. And that's all there is to it!'

And everyone marveled at the jurisprudential insight of this wisest of all Chinese.

Translated by John Dewey

The Fulfilment of Wishes

When the exceedingly wise and glorious great Emperor Yuan Hozan inherited power from his father, the Ruler of the Universe Huar Musian, and ascended to the throne of his ancestors, in accordance with the custom of our country the senior Master of Ceremonies approached him with a hundred bows and placed a basket made of simple rushes next to the throne.

"What is the meaning of this?" graciously enquired the youthful Son of Heaven.

"Master of the Universe," replied the Master of Ceremonies, "it is a tradition in our wise country to place this simple basket next to the Emperor's magnificent throne. During his lifetime the Emperor writes down his secret wishes on pieces of paper and drops them into the basket. While the Emperor is alive none may dare touch it. But when Heaven spirits him away from earth again, in other words when he is united with his ancestors, or to put it simply, when he dies, the papers are unfolded and read out before the people, and the late Emperor's wishes are carried out as a sacred duty."

"An excellent tradition!" said Yuan Hozan. "I should like to know the wishes expressed by my sacred ancestors."

"The Court Historian will answer your question impartially, O Grace of the Sun!"

And with many bows the Court Historian stepped forward, prepared to answer.

"Were many wishes found after the death of my great-grandfather, the great Tun Li Qisan, and of what nature were they?" asked the Emperor.

"Light of the Sun! Smile of the Heavens! When Heaven robbed earth and your great-grandfather ceased to be among us, as many notes were found in his basket as there were days in his just and glorious reign. And all exactly the same. Every evening before retiring to bed he wrote down the same secret wish."

"And what was it?"

"Your great-grandfather, the great Tun Li Qisan, was a wise and, most importantly, a just ruler. That was the virtue he strove after more than any other. Justice blossomed like a flower in his heart. And his only wish was this: 'Let the judges be just, wise, honest and impartial in their judgments.' When this wish was read out to the people, in accordance with hallowed tradition, all fell upon their faces and extolled the divine wisdom of the late lamented Emperor."

"And was his wish duly carried out?" enquired the Emperor.

"Master, Wisdom and Joy of the Universe!" replied the Court Historian, throwing himself to the ground. "It is not men but circumstances that govern this earth. The planets exert their influence upon the course of earthly affairs. There are evil as well as good dragons among those governing the world. The gap between intention and deed, said Confucius, is as great as that between good and evil. Men often appear to be mad or blind: they go left when they want to go right, and blunder over ruts and potholes when there is a straight road nearby. In a word, your wise great-grandfather's wish has not yet been put into effect."

"Then tell me, what were my grandfather's wishes?" Yuan Hozan was curious to know.

"The reign of your grandfather, the great A Po Qinian, was long and happy," replied the Court Historian. "He has gone down in history as A-Po Qinian the Unselfish. Whenever one of the viceroys incurred a fine to be paid into the imperial coffers as the result of some misdemeanor, the Unselfish preferred to chop off the culprit's head. He was not susceptible to treatment with metals as practiced by our Chinese medicine from time immemorial. The glitter of gold could never cure his anger, and when his notes were read, it became evident that only one sorrow had darkened his heart. It was his wise custom to note down his wishes every new moon. At the rising of each new moon your grandfather would confer with his soul, write down its secret wish and drop the paper in the basket. After his death as many notes were found as there had been moons in his reign. His soul was endowed with wisdom, and his wish was always the same: 'Let the mandarins not take bribes!'"

"Was this wish carried out?" asked Yuan Hozan.

"Master of the Universe!" exclaimed the Court Historian in reply. "The reign of his son, your sage father, was clouded by only one thing: that the mandarins took too many bribes!"

"Very well," said Yuan Hozan after a pause. "And my father, Huar Musian the Wise (may his name be glorified for all eternity): were many notes found after his death?'

"In your father's basket," replied the Court Historian, "only one note was found. Into that note he had poured the whole wisdom of his life. He had written: 'How I wish I was not Emperor!' He was the only Emperor whose wish was fulfilled. Since his death he has ceased to be Emperor."

"Very well!" said Yuan Hozan and, turning to the senior Master of Ceremonies, he commanded: "You may turn the basket over and take away the paper, India ink and brushes. I don't think I shall need any of that."

And all marveled at the young Emperor's wisdom.

Translated by John Dewey

On the Value of Learning

There once ruled in China an Emperor called Zan Liuo (may his name be preserved in people's memories for as long as our fatherland exists). He took a keen interest in scholarship, although he himself was scarcely able to read and always entrusted others with the signing of his name, something of which the mandarins in his entourage took much advantage.

But in spite of this Zan Liuo was still fascinated with

scholarship, to the extent that one day he asked himself the question: "What on earth is the point of its existence?" And he ordered all the scholars to be summoned on a certain day for public questioning.

The Son of Heaven's wish is law on this earth.

Huge drums were beaten at the gates of all the universities, and public criers shouted: "Hearken well, ye scholars! Leave your books and proceed to Peking, there to report to the Joy of the Universe, our gracious Emperor, what practical use, if any, your learning may have.'

On the appointed day all the learned men of China assembled on the great square before the palace. Among them were men so old that they had to be carried on stretchers; but there were also young scholars who seemed older than the oldest of those present. There were scholars with their heads held so haughtily high that their spines were bent backwards, making it impossible to bow should they even encounter a god. Others had the same curvature of the spine in reverse from prolonged bending over books. Some were laden with honors for their learning: scholars with three, four, in rare cases even five pom-poms to their cap. There were those who sported the three-eyed peacock feather. There were some scholars in green tunics, and even a few in yellow ones.

And of course all wore spectacles, for spectacles, as we know, are the surest indication of learning. Scholars are always short-sighted. When the sun came out from behind the clouds and glinted on these spectacles, the Emperor was even forced to screw up his eyes. "How their eyes burn!" he thought. "As if they were expecting a pay rise!"

Casting his gaze over the crowd and seeing that all was in order, the Emperor declared: "In never-ceasing concern for the welfare of our children the Chinese people, we have decided to seek an answer to the question: What is the reason for scholarship's existence? It has been with us since time immemorial, yet we should like to know: to what purpose? Therefore, answer directly and openly, without prevarication or cunning of any sort. What is the point of scholarship, what is its use? We may as well start with you." The Emperor pointed to a highly distinguished astronomer. "As the Son of Heaven myself, I desire to start with the Heavens. That will be most appropriate. Your science is the most elevated, so you shall speak first!"

The distinguished astronomer stepped forward, gave the number of bows dictated by protocol, and said in a gentle voice: "When for some reason an ignorant man has to leave his house at night, like a pig he only looks down at his feet, and if he should happen to glance up at the sky he sees only that it is studded with stars. Not so a learned astronomer! For him the patterns of stars are words, and he reads the Heavens like a book: should floods be expected, whether the tides will be great, how fiercely or weakly the sun will shine. All in all, we discern the future."

"The future? Very interesting!" said the Emperor. "But answer me this: what is happening now, at this very moment, in Nanxiong?"

"How may I know that, O Light of the Universe?" replied the astronomer, bowing humbly.

"A fine state of affairs!" exclaimed the Emperor. "The future you know, but not the present! You'd do better to know the present: that would be more useful! But you speak to me of the future! In my opinion your science is the most useless and stupid of all! Next!"

Standing behind the astronomer was a distinguished historian, said to be so accomplished in his field that he could name every Chinese who had ever lived. Prostrating himself before the Emperor, he said: "Model of the Virtues, Great Ruler whose equal in all the history of China even I do not know! My discipline will of course not arouse your wise anger as did that of my precursor. We investigate the past. We study it, marking well all blunders, mistakes and even acts of stupidity."

"A branch of knowledge Heaven-sent for fools!" exclaimed the Emperor. "It allows any fool to commit as many acts of stupidity as he wants with impunity! He has only to cite your subject as evidence, noting that mistakes and acts of stupidity have been committed throughout history! An idiotic subject! Away with you! What do you study, and of what use is your subject?"

The trembling scholar to whom this question was directed managed somehow to overcome his trepidation and replied: "We study questions of political economy: how the state should be governed, what sort of laws there should be, what rights should be enjoyed by mandarins and what rights by the common folk."

"Should? Should?" cried the Emperor. "As if in this world everything happens as it should! In this world things never turn out as they should. Willy-nilly, thanks to your subject, everyone will start comparing what is with what should be, and will always end up dissatisfied. A most harmful subject! Out of my sight! Get you gone! What do you have to say to us?"

This time the question was addressed to a doctor.

"Our science," replied the doctor, bowing, "is universally recognized as useful. We study the properties of herbs and what can be made from them: an extract from one, a powder from another, an ointment from a third. We gather ginseng roots, learning which to select, namely those most closely resembling the human figure. We dry the still young and soft antlers of deer, grind them up and make a broth from them, as thick as glue and as healing as spring air, that cures all ailments as if by magic. Of course, when people are well they have no need of our science, but if they neglect their health and fall ill we may help them.'

"Neglect their health? They should take care not to!" said the Emperor, his voice milder than before, yet still marked by anger. "You only encourage people to act irresponsibly. It is quite beyond me what use any of your specialisms are!"

And turning to the great and distinguished poet Mu Si, who was then living, the Emperor commanded: "Let us hear your answer as to the benefits of scholarship!"

Mu Si came forward, bowed and said, smiling: "One of your ancestors, O Son of Heaven, had a wonderful garden in which grew such marvelous sweet-scented flowers that not only did the bees from all around swarm there, but people even a mile or more away would stop, sniff the air and say: 'The gates of Heaven must have been left open today.' Then one day a cow blundered into the garden and, seeing a lot of strange things growing in the soil, began to eat the flowers. She started chewing a rose, but stopped when it pricked her tongue. She tried chewing lilies, nibbled at mignonettes and stocks, took a mouthful of jasmine, but spat it all out. 'No taste at all!' said the cow. 'I really don't understand it: why do people grow flowers?' As I see it, O Son of Heaven, the cow would have done better not to ask herself this question."

The Emperor flew into a rage and cried: "Off with his head!"

The executioners chopped off Mu Si's head there and then.

Looking at Mu Si's headless corpse, the Emperor began to reflect, and for quite some time remained deep in thought. Then at last he sighed and said: "There was only one clever man in the whole of China, and now even he is no longer with us!"

Translated by John Dewey

A Story about One Wet Nurse

The Chinese Emperor Dsing Li O, known as Hao Too Li san He Hoon which means "Justice Itself", awoke one day feeling ill. A rumor that the Emperor was sick spread through the palace. Many stopped to bow to the Prime Minister. The Court Poet composed a welcome ode to the Emperor's heir. The best doctors, white with fear, making genuflections and excuses, murmured in horror, and the Chief Physician prostrated himself and exclaimed, "Will I be allowed to speak the whole truth and nothing but the truth, O Consolation of Humanity?"

"Speak the truth," said the Emperor.

"You are the Son of Heaven," said the Chief Physician, "But sometimes, because of your unlimited mercy, you condescend to put yourself on a human level and it pleases you to be sick with the same sicknesses as ordinary mortals. Today is the day of your greatest leniency – you have a simple indigestion."

The Emperor was astonished. "Why is that? At night I drink nothing but the milk of my wet nurse. As an Emperor, I must be nourished by what becomes an emperor – the milk of wet nurses. I have had 350 wet nurses to date, but never have I had anything like this. What happened? Who and what made my wet nurse overeat?"

A strict investigation was immediately undertaken. The findings, however, showed that all the wet nurses ate the most delightful food, and that it was given to them in rather small quantities.

"Perhaps she was sick from the beginning," declared the Emperor. "Where were the eyes of the ones who selected her? Execute them!" he ordered in anger.

The guilty ones were executed, but after a careful investigation it was discovered that they were not guilty at all. The wet nurse was in perfect health. The Emperor summoned the wet nurse before him. "Why is your milk spoiled?" asked the Emperor sternly.

"Son of Heaven, Benefactor of the Universe, Justice Itself," answered the trembling wet nurse, "You look for truth not where truth hides. No one here made me overeat and I, by myself, did not overeat! I have never been sick from the day I was born. My milk turned bad because I think constantly about what is happening at home."

"What is happening at home?" asked the Emperor.

"I come from the province of Pe Chi Li, where it pleased you to nominate the mandarin Ki Hi as governor. He does terrible things, O Joy of the Universe. He sold our house and took the money for himself, because we could not pay him the bribes he demanded. Ki Hi took my sister as a concubine and executed her husband, so that he would not complain. And that is not all. He executed my father and jailed my mother. He acted with us as he acts with everyone. When I think of this, I start to cry and now my tears have turned my milk."

The Emperor became very angry. "Call all my advisors!" he shouted. And when the advisors appeared he sternly ordered, "Find an honest man!"

Such a man was found. And the Emperor said to him, "Mandarin Ki Hi, whom I put in charge of the province of Pe Chi Li, has created such havoc there that even the milk of my wet nurse is turning sour. Ride out to this province and in my name make a most thorough investigation and report back to me. But see that you report the whole truth, with nothing hidden, nothing added; truth shall be reflected in your words as the moon is reflected in a quiet sleepy lake. You know, on a quiet night you cannot tell where the real moon is – in the sky or in the lake."

The honest man left immediately, accompanied by a hundred experienced investigators. Frightened to death, Mandarin Ki Hi, who saw that the situation was very bad, offered the Emperor's envoy a large bribe. But the honest man, sent by the Emperor himself, did not dare to accept it. Three times the moon changed in the sky, and the honest man still continued his investigation. Finally by the end of the fourth month, the honest man appeared before the Emperor, prostrated himself, and asked, "Shall I tell you the whole truth, Justice Itself?"

"The whole truth," the Emperor commanded.

"There is not, in the whole universe belonging to you and only you, a little corner more worthy of tears than the province of Pe Chi Li, O Son of Heaven! Truly, even the most cruel dragon would shed tears there. Everyone in the province begs for alms, but no one can give because everyone asks. Houses are destroyed. Rice fields are not seeded, and not because the people are lazy, but because Mandarin Ki-Hi confiscates any money they earn. There is justice there – he is right who gives a larger bribe to Ki-Hi when being judged. Morals they don't even think about. It is enough for Ki Hi to see a girl he likes to take her from her father and mother. He takes not only maidens but even married women."

"It is impossible!" exclaimed the Emperor.

"Not only the moon, but even the sun could look into the truth of my words," said the honest man. "Everything I say is the truth, and nothing but the truth. Pe Chi LI, the ornament of your power, the flower of your provinces, is perishing."

The Emperor, with a sigh of deep sorrow, grasped his head with both hands. "We will have to think what to do! Yes, we must think." He ordered all the courtiers to wait in the great hall, while he himself went into the next room, and there he started to pace in deep reflection. The whole day passed. Before the evening descended, the Emperor returned to his courtiers and sat down on the dais under the canopy, and when everyone prostrated themselves before him, he solemnly stated, "The province of Pe Chi Li is in a terrible state. Therefore, we command that wet nurses for the Emperor of China never be taken from this province."

From that day on, wet nurses for Chinese emperors were never taken from the province of Pe Chi Li.

Translated by Rowen Glie

Magic Mirror

"Look, bring me a nice gift!" O Mati San said to her husband Ki-Kou, who, for the first time in his life, was going to the city.

When Ki-Kou returned, she met him with a question: "Where is your gift for me?"

Ki-Kou's business in the city was very good. He had

made some money and had returned with many useful household articles. "And for you, look here!" he said giving her a sparkling disk made of shiny metal.

O Mati San even cried in panic when, from the little frame in which the polished disc was encased, a pretty smiling female face looked back at her. "Who is this?" she asked in fright.

"Ha, ha, ha!" roared Ki-Kou. "Who is that? Why you, of course!"

"Ha, ha, ha!" laughed O Mati San with him, like a little silver bell. "How great is the wisdom of men!" exclaimed O Mati San, looking at herself in the mirror. "In the city they can draw portraits of people whom they never saw." Finding that the woman looking back at her from the mirror was very pretty, O Mati San declared that the portrait was very good.

From then on, the house of Ki-Kou began to resemble a cage in which lived a very lively bird. All day long O Mati San danced and sang, and looked at the wonderful portrait which smiled and rejoiced exactly like her.

But there is time for everything. Between amusement and play O Mati San gave birth to a daughter, O I San. Three people now composed the family. Some time was spent in work and worry. The wonderful, toy-like and most precious treasure was hidden at the bottom of a chest, and O Mati San devoted herself completely to work and the care of the family.

The daughter grew. It seemed that the life of O Mati San had been poured into O I San. The more gaunt and pale the cheeks of O Mati San became, the pinker the cheeks of O I San. When O I San reached the age of fourteen, Ki Kou could truthfully say, hugging them both, "Now I have two little Matis – an old one and a young one."

O I San looked exactly like her mother. Now it was

she who chirped in the small house made of paper, causing it to resemble a cage with a gay little bird.

But there comes a time for everything. Joy was coming and going away; work came, and death came, as it comes to everyone. O Mati San was dying. "Is it possible that I will never see you again?" sobbed O I San, heartbroken.

"My child!" answered O Mati San, you will see me any time you want. I will always be with you. And you will not see me as you see me now, old and sick, but you will see me as I was before, gay, young, smiling, and pretty, just as you are now." And with those final words, O Mati San joined her ancestors.

After mourning her mother, O I San remembered the portrait. She opened the trunk, took out the beautiful framed shiny disc which was hidden under the other things as a most cherished treasure, looked at it, and cried out in delight, happiness, and rapture. What looked back at her was her mother, not the old and sick one, but the young and full-of-life mother whom O I San remembered from her childhood.

O I San now spent entire days with the magic toy, admiring the beloved face of her dear mother. She talked to her, and though her mother never answered, O I San could tell from the way her lips moved, from her smile and the shine in her eyes that her mother understood her perfectly. When O I San was happy, her mother smiled also. When O I San was sad, sadness would cover the dear face, and O I San would smile in order to dispel the sadness in her dear mother's face.

One day, the very wise priest of the great goddess Kannoun passed through the village. "What are you doing, my child?" he asked, seeing that O I San was laughing and talking while looking into a mirror.

"I am talking to my dead mother," answered O I San. "I look at her face and I am happy when I see her so gay and happy."

"But is that your mother's face? You silly child!" said the wise priest, shaking his head. "Is that a portrait? No, it is a mirror, and it reflects your own face. See? Give me the mirror. I will look into it and it will reflect my face."

Frightened, O I San gave the mirror to the priest, and now she saw looking out of the beautiful frame the yellow, wise face of the priest. "It is not your mother's portrait, but your own," explained the priest.

"Mine?!" exclaimed O I San, as she fell sobbing to the ground. "I have lost my mother again!" And, lying on the earth, she sobbed inconsolably.

And the goddess Kannoun, the goddess of pity, said, "Cursed priest! Happiness is ignorance! Why did you have to poison a human being with your knowledge? Be cursed with all your knowledge!"

Thus was cursed the overly wise priest of Kannoun.

Translated by Rowen Glie

The White Devil

Wise Dung Sao was the most learned of men. He knew everything that happens on earth, beneath the earth, in the waters and among the stars. Calmly and without hurrying he now took the few steps separating him from the grave dug in his garden.

"Today I may still walk to it myself, but soon..." he thought each morning with a smile as he went to look at his grave. "I know a great deal, but there I shall learn all the rest!" And he would smile at the grave, which smiled back at him, surrounded by flowers.

One day as Dung Sao stood looking at his grave he was approached by the Spirit of Man.

"Wouldn't it be good to live one's life again!" said the spirit.

"But why?" exclaimed the wise man. "Standing at the threshold of his destination after a difficult and exhausting journey, only a fool would go back and repeat the whole thing again!"

'But wouldn't it be good!' the spirit replied.

"Man, like a marmot, scurries from his cradle to seek refuge in the grave. I have finished with this contemptible existence."

The spirit sighed and said: "But wouldn't it be good!"

Dung Sao went on to talk at length and with great wisdom about the vanity of human existence, about suffering, privation and disease; in reply the Spirit of Man merely sighed and repeated: "But wouldn't it be good to live again!"

"To know and constantly to desire more knowledge. And the more you know, the more you are tormented by this burning desire. Life is an ineffable torment! A constant thirst which only the grave can quench, and that in an instant!"

"But wouldn't it be good to live again!" sighed the Spirit of Man.

Concluding his deliberation, Dung Sao said with a sigh: "Indeed, it would be good to live one's life again!"

And in that same instant a devil appeared before him, its face whiter than white. It did not wear our sacred pigtail, and its short hair was blond and soft as silk.

"All hail, man of wisdom!" said the white devil.

'Before you, Dung Sao, other men are as grass before the venerable oak, and I am ready to serve you. I shall return your youth and fill your existence with all the joys there are to be had. I shall impart to you such knowledge and teach you such arts and skills that you will become a sorcerer, filling your own life and that around you with joy."

"But what price will you demand in return?" Dung Sao asked nervously. "My soul? My life?"

"No! Oh no!" exclaimed the white devil. "It's so much nonsense when they say we claim people's souls or their lives. That's all slander, pure ignorance. You will go through the whole of your life without fear or misgivings – but I shall always be walking one step ahead of you."

"Go then!" said the wise Dung Sao.

They set out through a dense forest overgrown with impenetrable thickets. The white devil walked in front, pushing the thorny briars aside so that Dung Sao might follow behind with ease and without scratching himself.

"What a fool this white devil is!" he thought, smiling to himself. "Let him always walk in front. That will be very good if we have to trudge through deep snow in winter or go somewhere with lots of trapping pits for wolves."

In this way they came at length to the lair of a mighty dragon. The dragon touched Dung Sao with its sting, and he was eighteen again. Not only had he himself grown young, but the whole world around him too. And in that world he saw many flowers imbued with delightful fragrances, while among the flowers birds darted, singing songs he had never heard as an old man.

And Dung Sao felt he wanted to turn the whole world into flowers. He found himself walking past the shop of a man whose skill it was to work precious stones into trinkets for the gratification of human vanity.

"I know miraculous arts and skills undreamt of by you!" said Dung Sao. "Allow me to work on your stones and I will transform them into wonderful flowers."

"By all means, if you are such an expert!" said the jeweler.

And since Dung Sao knew unusual arts and unusual skills, he gave the precious stones unprecedented forms. He set about fashioning flowers from each individual stone in turn. Massive diamonds blossomed into full-blown roses on whose petals the sun ignited fiery pin-points of gold, blue and red; large emeralds took on the contours of glistening leaves; from sapphires grew forget-me-nots.

Having labored at this task until evening, worn out from his exertions, Dung Sao went to his employer to receive his wage.

"A white fellow with hair like silk came by to collect your earnings for you," said the jeweler. "Just a moment ago – I'm surprised you didn't meet him going out!"

"There is no point in working if those are the terms!" grumbled Dung Sao, most put out by this, and he began to think instead only of pleasure.

And what should Dung Sao see coming toward him but a palanquin bearing a fourteen-year-old girl, daughter of the wealthiest and most illustrious mandarin. She was as beautiful as a fragrant unplucked blossom. So dainty were her feet that they seemed incapable of taking a single step and gave her a childish charm. Her future husband was lucky indeed: what joys would be his! Her timid, halting steps, like the first steps of an infant, would arouse delight and tenderness in his heart.

Her little eyes took in everything around her – trees, houses, people – with an expression of amazement, as if asking, "What is all of this?"

Such was her innocence.

Her tiny hands clung apprehensively to the sides of the palanquin, as if fearful that at any moment the wind might sweep up this flower of the earth and carry it into the air, refusing to return it to earth. In short, Dung Sao was much taken with her beauty. And because he was assisted by the white devil, or perhaps because Dung Sao was eighteen and handsome, the beautiful child's heart began to beat faster, stirred by desire.

The mandarin was only too delighted to give his daughter's hand in marriage to the most learned and proficient man in the whole country, and their wedding was celebrated with great splendor.

As the wedding feast drew to a close, Dung Sao took his leave of the guests to the accompaniment of immodest jests which only further inflamed his burning desire. He made his way to the bridal chamber, intending there, surrounded by flowers, to pluck the best of lilies and touch with burning lips the delicate scarlet flower of his bride's mouth. But at the entrance, he met the white devil coming out, who said: "I have done it for you!"

Dung Sao was racked with sobs, and the world seemed to him a garden in which flowers grew without fragrance and garish birds hopped pointlessly here and there without song.

So Dung Sao lived a life that was long, drawn-out and grey, until one day he found himself on the bank of a deep stream. A little bridge had been built across the stream, but so light and flimsy that only one person could ever use it. The first to walk across would make it so unsafe that anyone following would fall in the stream and drown. Just as Dung Sao was about to set foot on the bridge, the white devil squeezed past and crossed the bridge ahead of him. Dung Sao followed after, the bridge collapsed, and he was drowned, joyfully embracing death as deliverance.

There ends our tale.

Son of Heaven, beware white devils! They claim neither a man's soul nor his life, but they defile all that is best in the one and appropriate all that is good in the other.

Translated by John Dewey

Arabian & Other Tales

A Fairytale about a Fairytale

One day the idea of trying to get into the palace — the palace of Harun-al-Rashid himself! — came to Truth. Allah Akbar! By creating Truth a woman, You also created imagination!

And Truth said to herself, "And why should I not go? There are many houris in the Prophet's paradise, many beauties in the earthly paradise: the Caliph's harem. In the gardens of the Prophet, among houris, I would not be the last. And very possibly I would be the first among the Caliph's wives, and truly the first, among the odalisques in the Caliph's harem. Where are there corals redder than my lips? And their breath is like the hot air at noon. Slender are my limbs and like two lilies are my breasts – lilies with two drops of blood on them. Blissful is the one who rests his head on my bosom. Wonderful dreams will be his reward. My face is aglow with the radiance of the full moon. My eyes burn like black diamonds, and no matter how great the man who, in a moment of passion, looks deep into them, he will see himself so small, yes, so small that he must laugh at himself. In a moment of joy Allah created me, and I, the whole of me, am a song to my Creator."

And so Truth sallied forth, clothed only in her beauty.

At the palace gates, she was stopped by an indignant guard. "Woman who forgot to put on not only her veil, what do you want here?"

"I want to see the famous and mighty Sultan Harun-al-Rashid, the Padishah and Caliph, our great commander. Let Allah alone be our Master on earth," replied Truth.

"Let the will of Allah be in everything! What is your name? Shamelessness?" asked the guard.

"My name is Truth. I am not offended by you, warrior. The truth is as often taken for shamelessness as a lie is for shame. Go and announce me."

In the palace of the Caliph, upon learning that Truth had come, everyone became agitated.

"Her 'coming' means 'departure' for many of us," said Jaiffar, the Great Vizier. And all the Viziers sensed danger. "But she is a woman," continued the Great Vizier, "and it is our custom to put in charge of any business the one least capable. Therefore, it is the eunuchs who take care of women." He turned toward the Great Eunuch, the guardian of the Padishah's peace of mind, honor, and happiness, and said to him, "The Greatest of all Eunuchs! A woman has come who relies strongly on the power of her beauty. Chase her away. Remember, however, that this is a palace. Do this as it is appropriate at court, so that everything is gracious."

The Great Eunuch went to the gate and, looking with his dead eyes at the naked woman, addressed her thus: "You wish to see the Caliph? But the Caliph cannot see you as you are now."

"Why?" asked Truth.

"As you are now, people come into this world; as you are now, people may leave it. But people may not go about naked in this world," replied the Great Eunuch.

"Truth is only genuine when it is naked," she countered.

He defended his position: "Your words sound right, they sound like the law. But the Padishah is higher than the law. The Padishah will not see you. You are naked."

The war of words continued: "Allah created me naked. Be careful, Eunuch, to judge or to blame. To judge will be foolish; to blame, insolence," retorted Truth.

"I am not judging or blaming what Allah created," continued the Eunuch, "But Allah created the potato raw and so it is boiled before it is eaten. God created the meat of mutton full of blood, and so it must be fried before it can be eaten. Allah created rice hard as bone, and so it must first be cooked and sprinkled with saffron. What would people say about a man who would eat raw potato or mutton, and nibble raw rice, saying 'So Allah created them'? The same is true of a woman: in order to savor her nakedness, she must first be dressed."

"Potato, mutton, rice!" cried indignant Truth. "And what about apples, pears, and fragrant cantaloupes? Must you also change them, O Eunuch, before you eat them?"

The Eunuch smiled as only eunuchs and toads can smile. "We cut off the cantaloupe's rind, apples and pears are peeled. If you wish, we can do the same with you."

Truth hastily withdrew.

"With whom were you speaking this morning at the palace gates?" Harun-al-Rashid asked the guardian of his peace of mind, honor and happiness. "It seemed to me that you spoke very harshly."

"A woman, so shameless she came as Allah created her, wanted to see you," said the Great Eunuch.

"Pain gives birth to fear and fear gives birth to shame," said the Caliph. "If this woman is shameless, treat with her according to the law!"

"We obeyed your will before you put it into words," said the Great Vizier Jiaffar kissing the ground at the Caliph's feet. "We dealt with the woman in accordance with the law."

The Sultan looked at him with approval and said, "Allah Akbar!"

Allah Akbar! By creating woman, You also created stubbornness!

The idea of trying to get into the palace — the palace of Harun-al-Rashid himself! — came to Truth.

She donned a hair shirt, belted it with a rope, took a staff in hand, and went to the palace. "I am The Accuser," she said severely to the guard. "In the name of Allah, I ask to be brought into the presence of the Caliph."

The terrified guard (the guards were always terrified when strangers approached the palace) ran to the Great Vizier. "Again this woman!" he cried. "This time she has covered herself with a hair shirt and is calling herself 'The Accuser.' But, by my eyes, I recognize her as Truth."

The viziers became very excited and started shouting, "What disrespect to the Sultan, to come against our will!"

And Jiaffar said, "Accuser? This is the Great Mufti's domain." He called the Great Mufti and bowed to him. "Your sense of justice will save us. Treat with her piously and with courtesy."

The Great Mufti went to the woman, bowed down to the ground before her, and said, "You are The Accuser? Let all of your steps on the earth be blessed. When muezzin sings the glory of Allah from the minaret of the mosque, and all the faithful gather for prayers, you shall come too. I will bow to you and give you the sheik's chair with its beautiful engraving. Go ahead! Expose the faithful. Your place is in the mosque."

"I want to see the Caliph," she replied.

"My child! The state is a mighty tree, the roots of which are deep in the earth," replied the Great Mufti. "People are leaves which cover the tree and the Caliph is the flower blooming on the crown of this tree. The roots, the leaves, and the tree are all made for one purpose: so that the flower will bloom magnificently, exhale fragrance, and embellish the tree. This is Allah's creation! This is Allah's wish! Your words, the words of The Accuser, are truly the water of life. Let every drop of this water be blessed! But where did you learn, my child, that a flower is to be watered? In order for a flower to bloom you must water the roots. Go in peace and water the roots, my child. Your place is in the mosque, among the simple faithful. There you may expose and accuse."

With angry tears in her eyes, Truth left the soft-spoken and paternal Mufti.

That afternoon Harun-al-Rashid said to him, "This morning, Great Mufti, I saw you speaking to someone at the palace gates. You spoke softly with affection. But in the palace, for some reason, I felt a kind of disturbance. Why?"

The Mufti kissed the ground at the Caliph's feet and said, "Everyone was upset because this was a mad woman. She came dressed in a hair shirt and requested that you too wear a hair shirt. It is ridiculous to think that the Sovereign of Baghdad and Damascus, Beirut and Baalbek would walk about in a hair shirt! This would be to show ingratitude to Allah for all his gifts. Such an idea could occur only to a lunatic."

"You are right," said the Caliph. "If this woman is mad, one should treat her with pity. Then again, she must be prevented from harming others."

"Your words, Padishah, are commendations for us, your servants, because it is in that spirit that we treated with this woman," said the Great Mufti.

And Harun-al-Rashid looked at the sky with gratitude for sending him such good servants. Allah Akbar!

Allah Akbar! By creating woman, You created cunning! The idea of trying to get into the palace — the palace of Harun-al-Rashid himself! — came to Truth.

She ordered gleaming shawls from India, transparent silks from Brusa, gold embroidered fabrics from Smyrna. From the bottom of the sea she took yellow amber. She adorned herself with the feathers of birds so small they feared spiders, and were often mistaken for golden flies. She adorned herself with diamonds which looked like large tears, rubies which resembled drops of blood, pink pearls which were like the traces of kisses left on the body of one who is loved, and sapphires like fragments of the sky.

Then Truth went to the palace, merry and joyful, her eyes full of fire, telling marvels about all these things. A huge crowd followed her, listening with avid enchantment and pounding hearts to her stories. "I am a fairytale, as many-colored as Persian rugs, meadows in springtime, or Indian shawls. Listen! Listen to the music of the bracelets on my hands and feet. They sound like the golden bells in the porcelain towers of the Emperor of China. I will tell you all about him. Look at these diamonds. They resemble the tears which a beautiful princess shed when her beloved departed to the end of the world to seek gifts for her. I will tell you about her, the most beautiful princess in the world. I will tell you about a lover who left, on the bosom of his beloved, traces of kisses the same color as these pearls. And about her eyes which, at the moment of passion, would become huge and black like the night, or like these black pearls. I will tell you about their caresses on a night when the sky was as blue as this sapphire and the stars shone like a lacy wreath of diamonds.

At the palace, Truth addressed the guard. "I want to see the Caliph. Let Allah give him as many decades of life as there are letters in his name, and double it and double it again, because there is no limit or end to the generosity of Allah! I want to see the Padishah. I want to tell him about forests of palm trees, all laced with liana, where these little birds fly, birds that look like golden flies. I will tell him about the lions of the Negus of Abyssinia, about the elephants of the Raja of Jodhpur, about the beauty of the Taj Mahal, about the pearls of the King of Nepal. I am a fairytale, a many-colored fairytale."

Rapt by the stories the fairytale was telling, the guard forgot to announce her to the vizier. But the fairytale had already been noticed from a palace window. "There is a fairytale! A many-colored fairytale!" cried the people.

And Jiaffar, the Great Vizier, caressing his beard, said with a smile, "She wants to see the Caliph? Let her. Shall we fear a fairytale? The man who makes knives does not fear knives."

Then Harun-al-Rashid himself, hearing the joyful noises, asked, "What is it? What is going on outside and inside the palace? What is the meaning of this commotion? Why this noise?"

"This is the fairytale," replied the vizier, "that came dressed in miracles. The whole of Baghdad is listening to her. Everyone, from the very young to the very old, is utterly captivated. She has come to see you, Master."

"Allah shall be the only Master! I want to hear what every one of my subjects is hearing. Bring her to me," said the Caliph.

And all the carved, engraved, and ivory-inlaid doors swung open before the fairytale. The fairytale approached the Caliph, Harun-al-Rashid, who was surrounded by bowing courtiers and prostrated slaves. He greeted her with a warm smile. And Truth, dressed as a fairytale, stood before the Caliph.

The Caliph, Harun-al-Rashid, addressed her with a smile. "Speak, my child. I am listening to you."

Allah Akbar! You created Truth. Truth wished to get into the palace of Harun-al-Rashid himself!

Truth always gets what she wants!

KISMET!

Translated by Rowen Glie

Truth

Behind lofty mountains and primeval forests lived Queen Truth. The world was filled with tales of her. No one had ever seen her, but everyone loved her. Of her the prophets spoke and the poets sang.

The very thought of Truth put fire in men's blood. People dreamed about her. To some, she would appear as a girl with golden hair, tender, lovely, and gentle. To others, she would appear as a dark-haired beauty, passionate and impetuous.

The songs of poets reflected these dreams. They sang, "Have you seen how a ripe wheat field sways on a summer day, like a sea of golden waves? Such is the hair of Queen Truth. Like molten gold it flows from her naked shoulders and reaches below her waist. Her eyes shine like bright cornflowers in ripe wheat. Get up at night and wait for the first small cloud to redden, the harbinger of dawn, and you will see the color of her cheeks. Like an eternal flower that blooms and never fades, such is the smile on her coral lips. Truth, who lives behind the tall mountains and the primeval forests, smiles to all, always."

Others sang, "The waves of her fragrant hair flow like the dark night. Her black eyes sparkle like lightning. Her beautiful face is pale. This dark-eyed, dark-haired and impetuous beauty, who abides behind the primeval forests and the tall mountains, smiles only to the chosen."

A young knight, by name Chazir, decided to visit Queen Truth. Behind steep mountains, behind thickets of impassable forest, according to all the songs, stood a palace made of the blue of the sky with columns made of clouds. "Happy is the brave man who will not be frightened by tall mountains and primeval forests. Happy is he who, tired and sore, will reach the palace made of the blue of the sky, will fall on the steps of the palace, and sing his invocation. A naked beauty will appear to him. Only once did Allah see such perfection. Delight and happiness will fill the heart of this young man. Wonderful thoughts will enter his head and marvelous words will come from his lips. The forest will make a path for him, the mountains will bow their heads to him and make an even road for him. He will return to the world to tell of the beauty of Queen Truth. And listening to his inspired tale of her beauty, all the people who exist on the earth, without exception, will fall in love with Truth. All will love her, and her alone. She will be the queen of the earth, and herald a golden age for her realm. How lucky and fortunate is the one who will see her!"

Chazir decided to go and seek Truth. He saddled his milk-white Arabian horse, tied his embroidered belt tight, and donned his grandfather's golden sword. Bowing to the friends, women, and warriors who had come to admire the young hero, he said, "Wish me luck! I am riding off to see Queen Truth and to look into her eyes. On my return, I will describe to you her beauty." With those words, he spurred his horse and raced away.

The horse sped over mountains like a whirlwind, over paths too narrow for a goat, and fairly flew over chasms. After one week of this, Chazir's tired and exhausted horse brought him to the edge of the primeval forest. Small huts stood there and golden bees were buzzing in a hive. Here lived the sages who separated themselves from things on the earth so as to reflect on things in Heaven. They have been called, "The first guardians of Truth."

Hearing the sound of a horse's hoofs, they came out of their huts and happily welcomed the armed youth. The oldest of the sages and the most venerated said, "May Heaven bless every visit of youth to the wise men! The sky itself blessed you when you saddled your horse!"

Chazir dismounted, kneeled before the wise old man, and said, "The thoughts are the age of the mind. I am greeting the age of your hair and that of your mind."

The old man liked this respectful answer and replied, "The sky did already bless your intention: you came safely to us through the mountains. Surely it was not you who drove the horse over this goat path. It was the archangel who conducted your horse, holding it by the bridle. Angels with their wings supported your horse when it stretched itself to its whole length to fly over bottomless precipices. What good purpose has brought you here?"

Chazir replied, "I have come to see Queen Truth. The whole world is full of songs about her. Some sing that her hair is as bright as the gold of wheat; others, that her hair is as black as the night. But all agree on one thing: Truth is exceptionally beautiful. I want to see her, to tell the whole world about her beauty. Let all the people of the world fall in love with her!"

"A good intention! A very good intention!" said the old sage. "You could not do better than to come to us. Let your horse have a rest, come into our hut, and we will tell you all about the beauty of the queen."

"Have you ever seen Truth?" exclaimed the young man looking with envy upon the old one.

The sage smiled and shrugged his shoulders.

"We live on the edge of the forest and Truth lives far away in the depths of it. The road there is hard, dangerous, and impassable. And why should we, wise men, go there? Why do useless work? Why should we go to look at Truth when we already know how she should be? We have wisdom, therefore we know. Come, and I will tell you everything about the queen."

But Chazir bowed to the old man and put his foot into the stirrup. "I thank you, wise old man. But I want to see Truth with my own eyes!" He was already in the saddle.

The sage shook with indignation. "Stop! Do not move!" he cried. "What? How? You do not believe in wisdom? You dare think we can make an error? You dare not believe a sage? You are a brat, a puppy, a milksop!"

But Chazir raised his silk whip. "Out of my way! Or I will offend you with my whip as I have never offended my horse!"

The sages jumped aside and Chazir rushed away on his rested horse. He still could hear the farewells of the wise men: "Perish, you wretch!" "Let the sky punish your insolence." "Remember, you fool, remember at the hour of death, he who offends even one sage offends the whole world!" "Break your neck, you wretch!"

Chazir rode on and on. The forest was becoming denser

and denser. The tangled undergrowth gradually turned into a thick oak wood.

After a day's ride, Chazir came to a temple in the shade of tall leafy oaks. This was the magnificent mosque that only a few mortals had ever seen. Here lived dervishes who modestly called themselves "The Dogs of Truth." Others called them "The Loyal Guards."

When the noise of the horse's hoofs awakened the silent place, the dervishes and the top mullah came out to greet the young hero. Said the mullah, "Blessed is he who comes to the temple of Allah. And he who comes to the temple in his youth shall be blessed his entire life."

"Blessed," the dervishes chorused.

Chazir alighted from his horse and bowed low to the mullah and the dervishes. "Pray for the traveler," said he.

"From where have you come and where are you bound?" asked the mullah.

"The purpose of my journey is that I may describe to the people of the world the beauty of Truth," said Chazir.

The dervishes laughed when he told them how he had threatened the sages with a whip. "None other than Allah himself inspired you to raise your whip! You did well by coming to us. What could the wise men tell you about Truth? Only what their own minds have deduced. Lies! We know everything about Truth and what we know comes to us from Heaven. We will tell you all we know and you will have the most exact facts. We will tell you what our most sacred books tell us about Truth."

Chazir bowed and said, "Thank you, Father! But, I did not come to listen to someone's tales or to read what is written in holy books. This I could do at home. There was no need to exhaust myself and my horse."

The mullah frowned slightly and said, "Ah, ha! Do

not be stubborn, my boy! I knew you as a child. I knew you when I lived in the world, when you were so little that I often took you on my lap. I used to know your father, Gaffiz, and your grandfather, Amolek, I knew him quite well. A good man was he, Amolek. He, too, often thought about Queen Truth. In his house there was a Koran. But never did he open it. He was satisfied with what the dervishes told him about Truth. He knew that the same thing that was told to him was written in the Koran, and that was enough. Why read the book? Your father Gaffiz was a bit more sophisticated. When he thought about Truth, he would take the Koran and start to read it. He would read, and the reading would satisfy him. But you! You went even farther. You are that kind of a man! Even the book is not enough for you. You came to us. Good boy! I praise you. Come, I am ready to tell you all I know. Yes, ready."

Chazir smiled. "My father went farther than my grandfather. I will go farther than my father. I assume that my son will go farther than I. He will wish to see Truth with his own eyes. Is it not so?"

The mullah sighed. "Who knows? Who knows? Anything is possible! A man is not a tree. You look at a small shoot and you cannot always say whether it will be an oak, a pine, or and ash."

Chazir was already astride his horse. "If that is so, then I will be off. Why leave for my son to do what I can do myself?" And Chazir touched his horse.

The Mullah grabbed the bridle. "Stop! Infidel! How dare you go after all I told you! Ah, you unfaithful dog! Then you dare not believe either us or the Koran!"

Chazir gave spurs to his horse. The horse reared and the mullah jumped aside. With one leap the horse brought Chazir deep into a thicket, and after him flew the curses, cries, and howls of the dervishes. "Be cursed, ungodly one!" "Be cursed, vile offender!" "Do you know whom you insult when you insult us?" "Let burning nails stick into the hoofs of your horse at every step." "Let your stomach rot and your insides come out as snakes." Thus the dervishes cried, rolling in the grass in fits of fury.

Chazir continued on his journey. But the way was becoming more and more difficult, and the thickets more and more impenetrable.

Suddenly he heard a shout. "Stop!" Ahead of him, Chazir saw a warrior standing with a tightly stretched bow, poised to release a trembling arrow.

Chazir held his horse. "Who are you? Where are you going? Whence and why?" asked the warrior.

"And, who are you?" asked Chazir. "Who gave you the right to ask questions? Why do you want to know?"

"I have the right to know as a soldier of our great Padishah. My comrades and I have been charged with protecting this sacred forest. Do you understand? You are at an outpost called 'Outpost of Truth', established to guard Queen Truth."

Chazir told the warrior where he was going and why.

Hearing that Chazir was bound for the palace made of the blue of the sky, where Truth resides, the warrior called the other guards and his officers. "You want to know how Truth really looks?" asked the commander, admiring the expensive weapons and the beautiful horse as well as the military carriage of Chazir himself. "This is a noble aim, my boy, a noble aim! Alight from your horse and come with me. I will tell you all. Everything is written in the law of the Great Padishah, even how Truth should be. I will read it to you gladly. Later, you may go back to your people and tell them all."

"Thank you," answered Chazir, "But I want to see Truth with my own eyes."

"Listen," said the commander, "we are not your sages or mullahs or dervishes. We do not like to make long speeches. Now do as I say! Get down from your horse!" The commander brandished his sword, the guards their spears. The frightened horse pricked up its ears, snorted, and backed away.

Chazir plunged his spurs into the horse's sides, bent down low and whistled over their heads with his scimitar, crying, "Out of my way, if you value your life!"

Followed by cries and curses, Chazir flew through the dense thickets and stands of trees. Soon it was so dark, it was as if night had come during the day. Thorny bushes formed a wall, barring his path. The noble horse, tired and exhausted, no longer reacted to the whip and finally fell to the ground.

Chazir went ahead on foot through the forest. The prickly bushes tore his clothing. In the darkness of the primeval forest he heard the roar and thunder of waterfalls. He had to swim across stormy rivers. He exhausted himself fighting cold forest streams, and furious beasts. He walked without knowing when the day ended or the night began. He slept on humid and cold ground, all hurt and bleeding, in sheer agony, listening to the howls of jackals, hyenas, and tigers coming from the thickets around him.

For a whole week he roamed like this in the forest, when suddenly he staggered — as though lightning had struck him. Straight from the nearly impassable bushes he entered a clearing bright with the blinding sun. Beyond it stood, like a black wall, virgin pine trees. But in front, in the middle of a meadow covered with flowers, stood a palace which seemed to be built out of the blue of the sky. The steps to it shone like the snow on a mountain top. The sunlight went around the blue and covered it like a web with the golden lines of wonderful verses from the Koran.

Chazir's clothing hung on him like rags. Only his gold-engraved sword remained as before. Half naked, with his magnificent bronzed body exposed, he was now handsomer than ever before. Chazir staggered toward the steps, snow white as they were described in the ballads, and collapsed in complete prostration.

The dew that covered the fragrant flowers with diamonds soon refreshed Chazir. He stood up, once again full of energy, not feeling any pain from his wounds and sores, nor any tiredness in his arms or legs. Chazir started to sing, "I came to you through a virgin forest, through dense thickets, high mountains, and wide rivers. The impenetrable darkness under the clusters of pine trees was for me as bright as day. The interwoven tops of the trees seemed to me like a gentle sky, and stars shone from their branches. The roar of waterfalls was like the murmur of a brook and the howling of jackals sounded like a song in my ears. In the curses of my enemies I heard the tender voices of my friends, and the thorny bushes seemed to me a soft and delicate down. Why? Because I thought about you. Because I was coming to you. Come out! Come out, oh queen of the dreams of my soul!" And hearing the sound of slow steps, Chazir closed his eyes, afraid of being blinded by the sight of such resplendent beauty.

He stood with his heart pounding, and after a few moments of waiting, he dared to open his eyes. Before him stood a naked old hag. Her skin was dark and blemished with brown spots. It was covered with wrinkles and hung in folds. Her gray hair was thin and unkempt. Her eyes were dull and tearful. Her body was all bent and she could hardly hold herself upright even when leaning on a cane. Chazir shrank back in disgust.

"I am Truth," she said. The petrified Chazir was speechless with shock. She smiled sadly with her toothless mouth. "And you thought you would find a beauty? Oh, I was a beauty on the first day of Creation. Only once did Allah see such perfection. But eons upon eons have passed since then. I am as old as the world! I have suffered a lot! This does not make one younger, my hero. It does not!"

Chazir thought that he was losing his mind. "But all those songs about a golden or dark-haired beauty!" he moaned. "What shall I say when I return? Everyone knows that I went to see a beauty. Everyone knows Chazir will not return without keeping his word. They will ask me, they surely will ask, 'What kind of curls has she – golden as ripe wheat or dark as the night? Do her eyes shine like cornflowers or like lightning?' What shall I answer, 'Her gray hair is like clumps of wool and her red eyes are watering?'"

"Yes, yes, yes," said Truth "You must tell them all this. You must tell them how my wrinkled skin hangs in folds from crooked bones, how sunken are my cheeks, how toothless my mouth! And everyone, in disgust, will turn away from the ugly Truth. No one will ever love me. They dream of a marvelous beauty! In no veins will the blood run hot when thinking about me. The whole world – yes the whole world – will turn away from me."

Chazir stood before her, holding his head with his hands, looking at her with insane eyes. "What shall I say? What shall I say?"

Truth fell on her knees before him and, holding out to him her emaciated arms, she said in a beseeching voice,

"A lie!"

Translated by Rowen Glie

2 x 2 = 4½

With the Arabs, my friend, as you know, everything is invariably Arabian.

In the Arab equivalent of our State Duma known as the Dum-Dum, they decided it was about time they started actually making laws.

Returning from their encampments in the provinces, the elected Arabs compared notes on what they had seen and heard. One of them said: "The people don't seem very satisfied with us. One man hinted as much to me: he called us idlers."

The others agreed.

"I've heard similar remarks. They call us parasites."

"I was called a wastrel."

"I was pelted with stones."

And so they resolved to set about drafting laws.

"We must immediately promulgate a law the truth of which is evident to all."

"And which provokes no arguments."

"Which is acceptable to everyone."

"And because of which no one loses."

"A wise law which everyone will love!"

The elected Arabs put their heads together and came up with an idea:

"Let's pass a law that says twice two is four."

"That is true!"

"And it will give no offence."

Someone objected: "But everyone knows that twice two is four."

To which the others replied quite reasonably: "Everyone knows you must not steal, and yet there is a law spelling this out."

And so in formal session the Arab delegates enacted the following decree:

"It is hereby declared law, ignorance of which shall be no excuse, that at all times and under all circumstances twice two shall be four."

When they heard of this, the viziers (that, my friend, is what the Arabs call their ministers) were greatly alarmed. They went to the Grand Vizier, who was as wise as his hairs were grey. They bowed before him and said: 'Have you heard that those children of misfortune, elected Arabs, have started promulgating laws?'

The Grand Vizier stroked his grey beard and said: "I will stay on."

"And that they've already passed a law that twice two is four?"

The Grand Vizier replied: "I will stay on."

"Yes, but Allah knows where they'll end up. They'll pass a law that it is light by day and dark at night. That water's wet and sand is dry. And people will be convinced it is light by day not because the sun shines, but because those children of misfortune, elected Arabs, have ordained it so. And that water is wet and sand is dry not because Allah created them like that but by order of the delegates. People will come to believe in the delegates' wisdom and omnipotence. As for what they will come to think of themselves, only Allah knows!"

The Grand Vizier said calmly: "I hear all you say, and I will stay on.' Then he added: 'I shall stay on whether the Dum-Dum promulgates laws or not. I shall stay on whether there even is a Dum-Dum or not. Let twice two be four, one or a hundred: I shall stay on regardless, whatever happens – stay on for as long as it is the will of Allah."

Such was the expression of his wisdom.

Wisdom is clad in imperturbability as the mullah in his white turban. The anxious viziers for their part headed off to the Assembly of Sheikhs. That, my friend, is more or less comparable to our upper chamber, the State Council. When they arrived, they said:

"Things cannot be left as they are. The elected Arabs mustn't be allowed to assume such power in the land. You have to do something about it."

And there assembled a great conclave of the sheikhs, with the viziers in attendance. The first among the sheikhs, their presiding chairman, rose to his feet. Without bowing to anyone (such was his self-esteem), he declared:

"Honorable and learned sheikhs. Those children of misfortune, elected Arabs, have acted like the most cunning conspirators, the most pernicious instigators, the worst brigands and lowest of scoundrels: they have declared twice two to be four. In so doing they have harnessed truth itself to the achievement of their vile aims. What they are about cannot escape our wisdom. They wish to make the gullible population believe that truth itself speaks through their lips. Then, whatever law they pass, those gullible people will see it all as true, and will say to themselves: 'Well, this was decided by the elected Arabs who said that twice two is four.' In order to nip this villainous plan in the bud and cure them of any desire to meddle in legislation, we must repeal their law. But how is this to be done, when twice two is indeed four?"

The sheikhs sat in silence, their beards all pointing at the speaker. At last they turned to one old sheikh, a man of wisdom and a former Grand Vizier. "You," they said, 'are the father of the misfortune." (That, my friend, is what the Arabs call the Constitution.) "A surgeon who has made an incision must be able to heal it again. Give voice to your wisdom.

You managed the Treasury, compiled records of income and expenditure, spent your whole life surrounded by figures. Tell us: is there no way out of this desperate dilemma? Must twice two really always be four?"

The wise sheikh, former Grand Vizier and father of the misfortune, rose to his feet, bowed and said: "I knew you would ask me. Although people call me the father of the misfortune, notwithstanding their hostility toward me they always seek my advice in times of trouble. In the same way a man who pulls teeth gives pleasure to none, but when there is no other remedy for toothache he is sent for. On my way here from the warm seashore where I have been living, as I watched the crimson sun sink into the azure sea, gilding it here and there, I cast my mind back to all the records and accounts I once compiled and found that twice two can be anything you like, depending on the needs of the moment. It can be four, or more, or less. In some records and accounts twice two was fifteen, in others it was three, depending on what had to be proved. It was hardly ever four. At least I can't remember such an instance. Thus speaks life experience, the father of wisdom."

The viziers were beside themselves with delight, but the sheikhs were in despair. "Then what is arithmetic?" they asked. "A science or an art?"

After due consideration the old sheikh, former Grand Vizier and father of the misfortune, replied in some embarrassment: "An art!"

Turning in despair to the vizier in charge of learning throughout the country, the sheikhs asked: "By virtue of your position you are constantly in touch with scholars. Tell us, vizier, what do they have to say on the subject?"

The vizier rose to his feet, bowed with a smile, and replied: "They say: 'Whatever is your pleasure.' Knowing that I would have to answer your question, I sought out those scholars still in my employ and asked them: 'What is twice two?' They bowed and said: 'What you command it to be." And however much I asked them, I could get no answer but: 'Whatever is your pleasure' and 'Whatever you command'. Arithmetic has been replaced in my schools by obedience, as have all the other subjects."

The sheikhs were greatly distressed. They exclaimed: "That does credit, O vizier in charge of learning, both to the scholars still in your employ and to your judgment in selecting them. Such scholars will perhaps set young people on the right path, but they do nothing to resolve our dilemma."

And the sheikhs turned to the Sheikh ul-Islam. "Through your ministry," they said, "you are constantly in touch with the mullahs and close to the divine truths. So tell us the truth: is twice two always four?"

The Sheikh ul-Islam rose to his feet, bowed and said: 'Honorable and most distinguished sheikhs, whose wisdom is dressed in grey hair as the deceased in a silver shroud. Live and learn! There once lived in the city of Baghdad two brothers: god-fearing men, but human like the rest of us. Each had a concubine. The brothers, who always acted in concord with each other, had each taken a concubine on the same day, and on that same day the concubines had conceived from them. As the time drew near for them to be delivered, the brothers said to each other: "We want our children to be born not of concubines, but of our lawful wives." And they summoned the mullah to consecrate their marriages. The mullah rejoiced in his heart at the brothers' pious decision and gave them his blessing, saying: "I hereby seal your separate unions. Now you will be a single family of four persons." But just as he uttered these words the two brides gave birth. And twice two became six, for the family now consisted of six persons. This is what came to pass in the city of Baghdad, and this much is known to me. But Allah knows more."

The sheikhs heard of this real-life event with the greatest delight. Then the vizier in charge of the country's trade arose and said: "Twice two is not always six, however. The following took place in the glorious city of Damascus. A certain man, foreseeing that he would need some small change, went to a robber."

(The Arabs, my friend, having as yet no word for "banker", use the time-hallowed expression "robber".)

"He went to a robber," continued the vizier, "and asked him to change two gold piastres for silver. After deducting his commission the robber gave the man silver coins to the value of one and a half gold piastres. But as things turned out the man found he had no need for small change after all, so he went to another robber and asked him to change the silver coins back into gold. The second robber took the same commission and gave the man one gold piastre. So two gold piastres, changed twice, became one, and twice two turned out to be one. This happened in Damascus and, my dear sheikhs, it happens all over."

The sheikhs were overcome with unspeakable joy. "This is what life teaches us," they exclaimed. "Real life – never mind what those elected Arabs, the children of the misfortune, may say."

They put their heads together and decided: "The elected Arabs have declared twice two to be four, but life disproves their claim. Laws which have no bearing on life have no place in the statute book. The Sheikh ul-Islam says twice two can be six, while the vizier in charge of trade has shown that on occasion it can also be one. To assert its complete independence, the Assembly of Sheikhs decrees that twice two is five."

And they ratified the law passed by the elected Arabs, commenting: "Let no one say that we never ratify their laws." They changed only one word, replacing "four" with "five". The law now read as follows:

"It is hereby declared law, ignorance of which shall be no excuse, that at all times and under all circumstances twice two shall be five."

The matter went before the Conciliation Commission. (Such conciliation commissions, my friend, are to be found wherever there is a "misfortune".) There the most heated of arguments broke out. The representatives of the Assembly of Sheikhs said: "You should be ashamed of yourselves, quibbling over a single word! In the whole law only one word has been altered, and yet you kick up a fuss about it. How shameful!"

For their part the representatives of the elected Arabs said: "We cannot return to our Arabs without a victory!"

For a long time the wrangling continued. Finally the representatives of the elected Arabs issued an ultimatum: "Give way or we shall quit!'

After conferring, the representatives of the Assembly of Sheikhs said: "Very well, we will compromise. You say four, we say five. Let it be so that no one can take offence, whether on your side or ours. We'll meet you halfway. Let twice two be four and a half."

The representatives of the elected Arabs conferred among themselves:

"I suppose some sort of law is better than none."

"I suppose we've forced them to compromise."

"And we won't get any more out of them."

And they announced: "Very well, we agree."

And the Conciliation Commission of representatives of the elected Arabs and the Assembly of Sheikhs declared:

"It is hereby the law, ignorance of which shall be no excuse, that at all times and under all circumstances twice two shall be four and a half."

This was proclaimed by public criers at bazaars throughout the land, and everyone was delighted.

The viziers were delighted: "The elected Arabs have been taught to think very carefully, even about declaring that twice two is four."

The sheikhs were delighted: "They didn't get their way!"

The elected Arabs were delighted: "We forced the Assembly of Sheikhs to compromise!"

All these groups congratulated themselves on their victory.

And the country?

The country was highly delighted. Even the cats had a good laugh. Such, my friend, are the tales to be heard in Arabia.

Translated by John Dewey

The Caliph and the Dancing Girl

An edict was once issued: "For the glory of Allah, the One and the Omnipotent. For the glory of the Prophet, may He have peace and blessings. In the name of the Sultan and Emir of Baghdad, Caliph of all faithful, and the humble servant of Allah – Harun-al-Rashid – we, the chief mufti of the city of Baghdad, proclaim this truly holy edict. Let it be known to everyone! This is what, in agreement with the Koran, Allah did put in our heart: that the forgetting of Allah causes impiety to spread on the earth and kingdoms to perish. Nations are destroyed and people die because of dissipation, luxury, orgies, and self indulgence! But it is our wish that the smell of piety rise up to Heaven from our city of Baghdad, as the scents from our gardens rise to the sky and the holy calls of Muezzins soar from our minarets.

"It is through women that evil comes into the world! They forget the commandments of the law, modesty, and the rules of good behavior. From head to toe, they cover themselves with jewelry. Their veils are as transparent as smoke from a Turkish pipe. And if they do cover themselves with the costliest of stuffs, it is only to show to the best advantage the sinful beauty of their bodies. They turn their bodies, created by Allah, into instruments for temptation and sin. Tempted by them, warriors lose their courage, merchants their money, artisans their love for their trade, and peasants any desire for labor. This is why we have decided to remove the sting from the serpent.

"We proclaim to everyone who lives in the great and glorious city of Baghdad that dancing, singing, and music in Baghdad are hereby forbidden! It is forbidden to laugh and to joke. The women who must go out of their houses shall be covered from head to toe with a veil made of white cotton. The veil may have two small holes for the eyes so that women while walking on the streets have no excuse to bump into men. We make it known to all women, old and young, ugly and beautiful, that should they expose even the tip of their little finger, they will be accused attempting to bring perdition on all men and defenders of Baghdad, and will be stoned immediately.

"This is now the law! It shall be observed and obeyed

as if it had been signed by the Caliph himself, the great Harun-al-Rashid. Signed: Sheik Hazif, by the grace of the Caliph, the Great Mufti of the city of Baghdad."

On all streets, in all bazaars, and at all crossroads, heralds read the edict to crowds gathered by the roar of drums and the shrill sound of pipes. And from that very moment, in the merry and magnificent city of Baghdad, all singing, music, and dancing stopped. It was as if a plague had visited the city. Baghdad was as quiet as a cemetery. Like ghosts, covered in dead white from head to toe, women walked in the streets. Only frightened eyes could be seen through small slits cut in their veils.

People are always like this: when they rebel, they rebel for good, but when they start to obey the law, they obey it in such a slavish way that even the government in power becomes disgusted.

Harun-al-Rashid himself could not recognize his happy joyful Baghdad. He said to the Great Mufti, "Very wise sheik, it seems to me that your edict is too strict."

"Master! Laws and dogs must be mean in order to be feared!" answered the Great Mufti.

Harun-al-Rashid nodded to him. "Maybe you are right, very wise sheik."

At this time, in distant Cairo, town of laughter, jokes, luxury, music, singing, dancing, and transparent veils, there lived a dancing girl by the name of Fatima Chanum. Let Allah forgive her the pleasure she gave people. She had just reached her eighteenth spring. Fatima Chanum was famous among women dancers in Cairo, and women dancers in Cairo were famous among dancers the world over. She had heard much about the luxury and richness of the Orient, but the greatest diamond in the Orient was Baghdad.

The whole world talked about Harun-al-Rashid, the

great Caliph of all faithful, about his magnificence, splendor, and generosity. Rumors about him reached her pink ears and Fatima Chanum decided to travel east, to Baghdad, to Caliph Harun-al-Rashid, and gladden his eyes with her dancing. She said, "It is customary that each faithful brings to the Caliph the best that they have. I will also bring to my Caliph the best that I have: my dancing." She packed her dancing costume and set off for Baghdad.

A tempest met the ship on which she sailed from Alexandria to Beirut. Everyone on the ship lost their head. Fatima Chanum, however, calmly put on her dancing dress. "Look!" cried the frightened passengers pointing, "That girl has gone crazy."

But Fatima Chanum replied, "To make a living, a man must have a sword. A woman, however, needs only a dress which is becoming to her. A man will then give her anything she needs."

Fatima Chanum was as wise as she was beautiful! She knew that everything is already written in the Book of Fate. Kismet!

The vessel was thrown against some rocks and splintered to pieces. Of all the passengers, Fatima Chanum alone was cast by the waves onto the shore.

In the name of Allah, she sought and was granted help from a passing caravan traveling from Beirut to Baghdad. The camel driver said to her, "Do you realize that we are taking you to your death? In Baghdad, because of your dancing costume, you will be stoned."

"In Cairo," retorted Fatima Chanum, "I was dressed as I am now and no one touched me, even with a flower."

"But the Cairo mufti is not as virtuous as Baghdad's Sheik Hazif," said the camel driver. "And no one in Cairo issued such an edict as in Baghdad!"

"Why did they issue that edict?" she asked.

"Because," replied the camel driver, "they say that such a dress inspires lustful thoughts in men."

"How can I answer for someone else's thoughts?" said Fatima Chanum. "I answer only for my own."

"Tell that to Sheik Hazif," he replied.

It was night when Fatima Chanum arrived in Baghdad. Alone and lost, she wandered in the streets of a dark, empty, and dead city, until she saw a house from which light was shining. She knocked. This was the house of the Great Mufti. Thus quails, during their winter flight south, are pushed by the wind straight into a net.

The Great Mufti did not sleep. He was sitting at his desk thinking about virtue and devising another edict even sterner than the first. Hearing a knock at the door, he became alarmed. "Is may be Caliph Harun-al-Rashid himself," he thought. "When he cannot sleep he likes to walk about the city."

The mufti opened the door himself then stepped back in amazement and horror. "Woman? Woman! In my house? At the house of the Great Mufti? Dressed like this!"

Fatima Chanum bowed reverently and said, "Brother of my father! I see by your noble appearance and your venerable beard that you are not a simple mortal. By the tremendous size of the emerald which is the ornament of your turban, the color of the Prophet, I guess that I see before me the greatest of all muftis, the Great Mufti of Baghdad, the venerable, the famous, and the wisest Sheik Hazif. Brother of my father, let me in as you would let in the daughter of your brother. I was born in Cairo. My mother called me Fatima. I am a dancer by trade, if this pleasure could be called a trade. I came to Baghdad to cheer with my dancing the eyes of the Caliph of all faithful. But I swear to you, Great Mufti, that I knew nothing about the severe decree which must be just since it comes from your wisdom. But this is why I dared come before you dressed not in accordance with the law. Forgive me, great and wise mufti!"

"Allah alone is great and wise!" answered the mufti. "My name is truly Hazif, people call me 'Sheik' and our great master, Caliph Harun-al-Rashid, nominated me, above my merits, to the rank of Great Mufti. It is your luck that you happened to come to me and not to a simple mortal. A simple mortal, obeying my edict, would be obligated to call the police or to stone you himself."

"Then, what will you do with me?" Fatima Chanum cried out in terror.

"I? Nothing! I will admire you. The law is like a dog: it must bite strangers and be affectionate to its master. The edict is very stern! But it is I who wrote it. Make yourself at home, the daughter of my brother. If you want to sing, do so. If you want to dance, do so!"

However, when the Great Mufti heard the sound of tambourines, he winced. "Hush! Someone may hear it!" And what will happen if the cursed magistrate learns that a foreign woman passed the night in the grand mufti's house? Oh, these civil servants! A serpent does not bite another serpent, but a civil servant has only one thought in mind: how to poison another civil servant. Indeed, this woman is beautiful. With great pleasure I would make her the first dancer in my harem. But, have wisdom, Great Mufti; wisdom! It would be best to send this sinful woman before the judge. Let her dance for him. If the magistrate declares her guilty, let justice be done. Not one person has yet been punished for disobeying my edict; a law not yet used to punish a transgressor is a dog that does not bite. People stop fearing it. But, should the judge decide to pardon her, the poison of this serpent will be pulled out! The one who accused of the same crime committed by the judge may sleep in peace."

So the Great Mufti wrote to the magistrate: "Great Judge! To you, as the superior magistrate of Baghdad, I send a criminal, a violator of my law. Like a doctor who examines a most dangerous sickness without fear of contracting the sickness himself, examine the criminal act of this woman. Look at her and watch her dance. If you find her guilty of breaking the law, let justice be done. If you find her deserving of an indulgence, call pity into your heart, because pity is higher than justice. Justice was born on earth, but pity was born in Heaven!"

The great magistrate also did not sleep. He was busy writing decisions for the cases he would hear only the next day, for it would be cruel to make the defendants wait long for their sentences. When Fatima Chanum was brought to him, he read the note of the Great Mufti and said, "Aha! The old scoundrel! He obviously broke his own law himself and hopes that I will do the same." Turning toward Fatima Chanum, he said, "And so, you, a stranger, seek justice and hospitality. Good! But, in order to perform an act of justice I must know all your transgressions. Dance! Sing! Perform your criminal acts. But remember one thing: nothing must be hidden from the judge! On this depends the justice of his verdict. As to hospitality, this is the true specialty of a judge; a judge always keeps his guests much longer than they wish to remain." And thus, on this night a tambourine was heard in the house of the chief magistrate of Baghdad. The Great Mufti had not made a mistake. He knew his judge.

That night, Harun-al-Rashid could not sleep either and, as usual, he spent a sleepless night wandering the streets of Baghdad. The heart of the Caliph was heavy. Was this his merry, noisy, careless Baghdad which never went to sleep until long after midnight? Now, only the sound of snoring could be heard from all the houses. Suddenly, the Caliph trembled. He heard the sounds of a tambourine. Strangely enough, the sounds of music were coming from the house of the Great Mufti. Then music sounded from the house of the chief magistrate. "Everything is perfect in our most perfect city," the Caliph cried with joy. "While vice sleeps, virtue enjoys itself." Harun-al-Rashid returned to his palace very much intrigued by the night's happenings in the houses of the mufti and the magistrate.

Impatiently, the Caliph waited for dawn. As soon as the pink rays of the sun poured over Baghdad, the Caliph went to the Hall of Lions and declared the Highest Court of Justice open. Harun-al-Rashid was seated on his throne. His armor bearer, the guardian of his honor and power, stood at his side holding a naked sword. On the Caliph's right sat the Great Mufti wearing his turban with the huge emerald, green as the color of the Prophet, may peace and blessings be his! On the Caliph's left sat the judge, a ruby of enormous size, the color of blood, adorning his turban.

The Caliph put his hand on the naked sword and said, "In the name of Allah, the only One and Merciful, I declare the Highest Court of Justice open. Let the court be as just and as merciful as Allah! Happy is the city that can sleep in peace because its rulers do not sleep. Last night Baghdad slept in peace, but three persons with high responsibilities did not sleep: I, the Emir and Caliph of Baghdad, my very wise mufti, and my fear-inspiring judge.

Said the mufti, "I was composing a new edict."

Said the judge, "I was busy with affairs of state."

But the Caliph answered gaily, "How nice it is to be busy with virtue, particularly when it is accompanied by the sounds of a tambourine."

"I was questioning a female criminal," said the mufti.

"I was questioning a female criminal," said the judge.

"A hundred times must a city be happy when crimes are prosecuted even at night," said the Caliph with a smile. "We too have heard about this 'criminal.' We heard about her from a camel driver in a caravan we met last night, and with whom the 'criminal' came to Baghdad. We ordered her arrest and she is here now. Let the accused come in!"

Fatima Chanum entered. Her body was shaking from fear and she fell down before the Caliph. The Caliph said to her, "We know who you are and we know that you came to Baghdad to gladden the eyes of the Caliph with your dances. The best that you have, you brought to us, in the childish simplicity of your soul. But you have violated the law of the Great Mufti, and for this you must be brought to justice. Get up, my child! May your wish to dance before the Caliph be fulfilled. If, after seeing your dances, the Great Mufti and the wise judge did not perish, then, with the help of Allah, the Caliph will not perish either."

And Fatima Chanum started to dance.

Looking at her, the Great Mufti murmured just loud enough to be heard by the Caliph, "Sin! What a sin! She is trampling our sacred law!"

Looking at her, the great judge murmured just loud enough to be heard by the Caliph, "Oh, criminal, criminal! Each one of her movements merits death!"

The Caliph watched in silence. At the end of the dance, the Caliph said, "Sinner! You came from a city of beautiful vice, Cairo, to strict and virtuous Baghdad. Here piety reigns. Piety, not hypocrisy. Piety is gold, but hypocrisy is token money for which Allah will not give anything except punishment and ruin. Neither your beauty nor all the misfortunes you suffered will soften the hearts of your judges. Virtue is stern and pity is unknown to it. Do not ask for pity from the Great Mufti, from the judge, or from your Caliph. Great Mufti, what is your verdict for this woman who broke the sacred law?"

The Great Mufti bowed and said, "Death!"

"Great judge, what is your verdict?"

The chief magistrate bowed and said, "Death!"

"My verdict too is 'death'!" said the Caliph. "You violated the holy edict and must be stoned right here, right now! Who will throw the first stone? I, the Caliph! I must throw the first stone that comes to hand." And Harun-al-Rashid took from his turban a diamond of truly tremendous size, the famous "Great Mogul," and threw it at Fatima Chanum. The diamond fell at her feet.

"You are next," said the Caliph to the Great Mufti. "Your turban is adorned with a magnificent dark green emerald, the color of the Prophet, may we all have peace and blessings. Is there a better destination for such a beautiful stone than to punish a vice?" The Great Mufti took off his turban, tore from it the huge emerald, and threw it at Fatima Chanum.

"Now," said the Caliph, "it is your turn, Great Judge! Your duty is stern, but with blood does the big ruby shine on your turban. Do your duty!" Silently, the judge removed his turban, tore out the ruby, and threw it at the girl."

"Girl," said Harun-al-Rashid, "take these stones, the punishment for your crime, and keep them in memory of the kindness of your Caliph, of the piety of his Great Mufti, and of the justice of his chief magistrate. And now, go!"

It is from this tale that the custom was born: to give beautiful gems to beautiful women.

"Sheik Hazif, my Great Mufti, I hope that today you will eat your pilaf with pleasure because I fulfilled your law," said the Caliph to the Great Mufti.

"I will," said the mufti. "But I am repealing my edict. It is too severe."

"What? Did you not say that a law is like a dog: the meaner it is the more feared it will be?" asked the Caliph.

"Yes, my master," replied the mufti, "But a dog must bite strangers. When a dog bites its owner, such a dog must be put on a leash or a chain."

So judged the wise Caliph Harun-al-Rashid for the glory of Allah, the only One and Merciful.

Translated by Rowen Glie

Ḫow Ḫassan Lost his Pants

"Yes, indeed!" said the old minstrel. "This tale is about how Hassan lost his pants."

In the great and famous city of Baghdad there lived a very rich and noble merchant. What was his name? When he was playing on his mother's lap (where is paradise if not on one's mother's lap?) his mother called him, "Hassan-Hakki – Hassan the happy one."

Hassan was young, handsome, smart, and rich – tremendously rich. What else could he wish for? Hassan wished to be married. No sooner said than done! For a bride, his friends found him the most beautiful girl in the whole city. She was… She was… No! There are no words to describe her beauty. She was so beautiful that only music could describe her. In other words, she was as beautiful as your own beloved, Sir. And as yours, my friend Abdullah, and as yours, my good master Ali. (In this way, I hope, we will satisfy all tastes.)

To his wedding, Hassan invited the whole city of

Baghdad. Here we must give credit to Baghdad's cooks: they proved themselves the finest in the whole world. A rumor went round the sheep herds of Baghdad: the end of the world had come! Hassan has decided to slaughter all the ewes, to have them filled with peanuts and fried.

Seeing this rich and magnificent wedding, women cried sweet tears because they ate too much pink Turkish delight, too many sherbets, and honey scented jams made of almond, peach, and apricot flowers. The young maidens ate only candied violets and lilacs, and swore not to eat anything else till their own wedding day. People were dizzy from the music, falling off their feet from all the dancing. Even wine, generally forbidden by the Koran, was served at this wedding. It affected the middle-aged solid citizens by going to their toes; they stumbled and tumbled on top of one another as if thrown down by an invisible force.

Finally, the clock struck midnight – the delectable hour! The women led the bride to the beautiful bedroom. With laughter and jokes they undressed her and made her lie behind a curtain of lace on the bridal bed. The best man went to get Hassan. Accompanied by his friends, Hassan went to the bedroom in a manner becoming to a young man of the world. His strides were sprightly, even vivacious, but without undue haste, for a wise man is never hasty, be he on his way to his execution, or to his wedding. Besides, life flies as fast as an arrow. There is no need to hasten the process of living.

And so, patiently and without haste, Hassan took a seat on a divan before the bridal bed which was enclosed in curtains of lace. He accepted the congratulations of his friends, and without haste he stood up and said, "I thank you, friends of my youth, and I say good-bye to my former life as a bachelor." Slowly, he stepped toward the bed. But... At that very moment, his pants fell down.

A roar of laughter like thunder filled the room. The old women cackled as if someone had tickled their throats. The laughter of the girls was like silver bells. The men rolled on the floor in convulsions of laughter. The bride, peeking out from behind the laces, trilled with laughter, then began rattling her rings and bracelets to disguise the sound. All the guests nearly died laughing. Hassan stood helpless with his naked legs and his pants lying about his ankles. Even his legs turned red from embarrassment.

Without realizing what he was doing, he pulled up his pants and ran out of the house. He ran into the courtyard, jumped on the first saddled horse he saw (it belonged to a guest), and flew down the street. Behind him, he could still hear the mad laughter coming from his house. Often a man's entire happiness depends on a trifle. Nearly insane, Hassan drove his horse faster and faster. He rode through the night, and by dawn had reached the city of Damascus.

They say that the bread of exile is bitter. This is a lie! Neither bitter nor sweet is the bread of exile. There is no bread for the exiled! There is no taste in the bread of exile. Like a beggar without a penny in his pocket, Hassan found himself on the street of a foreign city. In foreign lands the dogs at each gate are ready to attack a stranger as a thief. Only the trees in a foreign place meet one with hospitality, tending to one their leaf-covered branches as if to say, "Hang yourself!"

Hassan looked with horror on the foreign city. He went to the market where he sold his tired horse and bought a sack of fried almonds. He put his sack on his shoulders and went through the town, stopping before each window with the wooden grating of a harem – women's quarters. And there he would sing out, "I am a man come from afar! I am looking for women's teeth as white as my almonds. Hey! Where are the women with the whitest teeth?"

The women would smile and answer, "But, will we not break our teeth on your almonds?"

"Do not worry, my lady," answered Hassan. "My almonds will burst with envy the moment they enter your mouth. They will see the whiteness of your teeth and will crack from envy. You will not need to bite into them."

By noon, Hassan had sold all his almonds. He counted his earnings and bought oranges with red pulp. Continuing on his way, he now called out, "Where are the red lips as red as my oranges?"

And the women answered, "But are they juicy, your oranges?"

"Oh my mistress," replied Hassan, "My oranges will become tears when they will find themselves between your red lips!" The sun was still high in the sky when the oranges had all been sold.

Hassan also sold loads of Turkish delight and sherbet. He became known in the market. He received credit. He started to sell jewelry. On Mondays when, in accordance with Oriental law, only women go to the market, Hassan would place his wares around him and, smiling through his black beard, he would say, "My beautiful lady, or beautiful mistress! Buy these earrings. Do you see these diamonds? True tears! Tears are the ornament for a woman. Such is their fate! Kismet! Buy these earrings and tears will never shine in your eyes. Bribe your destiny! Why would tears shine in your eyes when they could shine in your ears?

"Oh beautiful mistress! Incomparable mistress. Do not buy anything! Only look. From your look this turquoise will become like a piece of the sky! Tell your beloved to buy this turquoise brooch. Let him see a piece of sky on the bosom of his beloved!

"Here is a sapphire – blue and deep like the sea! And

here is a ruby – red like a drop of blood! It shines even in darkness. Ask your beloved to buy you the sea or a drop of blood! My advice: buy the drop of blood. There is more tempest in a drop of blood than in the bottomless sea.

"Beauties, my beauties! Pearls! Here are pearls!" Hassan would cry.

"I am afraid. Do not pearls mean tears?" the women would ask.

"Only the small ones, my lady," Hassan would reply. "Only a small pearl brings tears. A large pearl has never yet made a woman cry!"

And so, with laughter and jokes, but always with good humor, Hassan ran his business, and soon he became rich and famous throughout Damascus. The talk about him reached the ears of the Sultan of Damascus himself. (Only Allah is the Sultan! There are no sultans except the Sultan of Sultans, Allah!)

The Sultan of Damascus wanted to see the man beloved by everyone. After conversing with Hassan, and thoroughly satisfying himself with Hassan's reasoning, the Sultan said to him, "The most difficult thing for a sultan is to select a vizier."

"You must know better, my master," said Hassan, "but to me it does not seem to be too difficult. Usually it is done like this: some man is nominated as a vizier. Because he was nominated a vizier, everyone starts to think that he is a clever man and we say, 'Here is a clever man. Obey him or off with your head!' But what if this were done differently? Let us not nominate a man to be clever and be a vizier, but take the cleverest man possible and nominate him to be a vizier."

The Sultan only shook his head. "That seems very simple. The thought never entered my head. Take a clever man and make him a vizier? Ah! Hassan! You are a clever man and I make you my vizier."

"Master! To listen to you is to obey!" replied Hassan. And Hassan became the great vizier. He was wise, good, and just. The good people loved him; the bad feared him. The laws that he issued were liked by everyone. And with amazement the whole of Damascus would say, "What kind of vizier do we have? Not of noble origin, not glamorous, not famous – just a clever man!"

Thus, ten years passed. One day, the Sultan of Damascus summoned his beloved vizier and said, "Hassan, blessed be the day when the wind tore you off your native tree and brought you here. Blessed be our great and holy Koran that orders us to be good to strangers! It is ten years that I have listened to your advice and done what you said for the good of my Damascus. Now, I want you to listen to me and do what I say. Listen, Hassan! Not for too much longer will I be able to listen to your good advice. The road to my grave is so short that I will have no time to look back. I see my native Damascus happy under your wise government and I want to preserve for it this happiness until the end of your days. Listen, Hassan! I have no heir. I will marry you to my daughter and I will make you the Sultan of Damascus. Listen and obey!"

Hassan kissed the ground at the Sultan's feet and said, "To listen is to obey. Sultan! Allah is the only Sultan. There are no sultans, except the Sultan over Sultans. And this is what the Sultan of Sultans told me: 'Hassan, beautiful is Damascus, but your native city is Baghdad. There are many beautiful women in the world, but no face of a beautiful girl is more charming than the wrinkles on the face of one's mother. The one who thinks that it is better to be a sultan in a foreign land than a simple citizen of his own land is not worthy to be a citizen of his own land or the sultan of a foreign land.'

So said to me the Sultan of all Sultans, and when the Sultan of all Sultans talks, the Sultan on earth must remain silent."

The Sultan became very angry. "Is this how you, a servant, obey your master? I wanted to make you happy and I will. I will do as I have decided!"

This illustrates the weak point of all sultans: they think that they can make people not only rich, strong, and noble, but also happy. In order to make Hassan happy, the Sultan ordered his arrest.

But Hassan ran away. He saddled his horse, put gold in his money belt, and at midnight he rode to Baghdad. As it was ten years since he had left, he did not give any rest to his horse, and when the sun's rays burst over the mountain, Hassan saw before him the gates of Baghdad. It seemed to Hassan that nowhere in the world did the trees bloom more beautifully and exhale a finer fragrance than in Baghdad. And nowhere in the world were minarets so tall and flying off into the sky. He dismounted from his horse, fell to his knees, and kissed the ground.

At this moment, an old beggar woman was sitting at the city gates and combing the insects from the hair of her granddaughter. "Look, Grandmother, look what that man is doing! Is he eating the dirt?" asked the little girl.

"He is not eating the dirt, he is kissing it," replied the grandmother. "Now be quiet. That is not your business. Maybe this man loves his native land or maybe he is drunk. But you must not speak to him. You should be ashamed of yourself. After all, you are not such a little girl."

"And how old am I, grandmother?" asked the girl.

"How old are you? Eleven years old. You were born the same year that Hassan the merchant lost his pants on his wedding day."

It was as though his native land had spat in his face.

Hassan jumped up. "Allah Akbar! Oh Allah, the Great, the Charitable, and the Gracious! They count the days from the time I lost my pants! Even a miserable girl, who does not know her own age, knows that eleven years ago Hassan lost his pants. I lived two lives. From a beggar I became a rich man. I was at the pinnacle of power, I ruled a city, I issued wise laws, I made a city prosperous and happy, I could have been a sultan. But here, even a beggar woman combing lice from the hair of her unwashed granddaughter cannot forget that eleven years ago I lost my pants."

Hassan jumped back on his horse and rode away. This is what Hassan had learned: that what is important is forgotten, while what is of no importance is remembered. Everything about people is known only to Allah.

Translated by Rowen Glie

Man

One day Allah came down to earth dressed as the most ordinary of men. He walked into the first village he saw and knocked at the door of Ali, the poorest man in the village. "I am tired, and I am dying of hunger," said Allah with a deep bow. "Take in a traveler."

Poor Ali opened the door to him and said, "A tired traveler is a blessing in a house. Come in." Allah entered.

Ali's family was seated at the table having supper. "Please sit down," said Ali. Everyone took a bit of food from his dish and gave it to the guest.

When they had finished eating, the family stood up to say a prayer.

Only the guest remained seated and did not pray. "Why do you not wish to pray to Allah?" asked Ali.

Allah smiled. "Do you not know who your guest is?"

Ali shrugged. "You said that your name is Traveler. How shall I know you by another name?"

"Well, know then that the traveler come into your house is Allah." And Allah started to sparkle like lightning.

Ali fell on the floor before Allah and cried with tears of joy, "Why has such a favor been bestowed on us? Are there not enough rich and famous men in this world? In the village we have a mullah, and Kerim, the elder, and we have Mahomet, the rich trader. But you chose the poorest man, Ali! I thank you!" Ali kissed Allah's feet.

Since it was late, everyone went off to bed. Only Ali could not fall asleep. He tossed and turned and thought the whole night.

The next day he went on thinking. Absorbed in his thoughts, he could eat no supper. Finally, Ali could stand it no longer. "Do not be angry with me, Allah." He said. "I want to ask you a question."

Allah nodded and gave his permission. "Ask."

"I am amazed," said Ali. "I am amazed and utterly perplexed. We have a mullah in our village, a man of great learning and fame. Everyone bows to him when they meet him. We have the elder, Kerim, a man of great importance – even the governor stays in his house when he passes through our village. We have a trader, Mahomet, a man so rich that there can be very few like him in the whole world. He could regale you with tales and put you to bed on pillows of pure down. And what do you do? You come to Ali, the poor beggar. You must like me, Allah, is it not so?"

Allah smiled and answered, "I like you."

Ali started to laugh with joy. "I am so happy!"

That night Ali slept happily. Happy, he went to work, and still happy, he came home, sat down to his supper, and happily said to Allah, "I have to talk to you, Allah, after supper."

"Let's talk after supper," Allah replied cheerfully.

When supper was over and Ali's wife had cleared the table, Ali said gaily to Allah, "You must like me very much, Allah, if you decided to come to me and not to someone else. Is it not so?"

"Yes," answered Allah with a smile on His face.

"It must be so!" continued Ali with a laugh. "There is a mullah in the village to whom everyone bows, there is the elder in the village who receives the governor when the governor rides through the village, there is this rich man, Mahomet, who would put pillows up to the ceiling for you and who would be glad to fry ten sheep for your dinner. And instead you come to me, to poor Ali! You must like me very much! Tell me, tell me how very much."

"Yes, yes," answered Allah with a smile.

"No, you tell me how much you actually like me," pressed Ali. "Do not keep saying 'Yes, yes,' but tell me exactly how much you like me."

"Yes, yes, yes! I like you very, very much," answered Allah with laughter, "Truly very much."

"Very well, Allah, let's go to sleep."

The next morning, Ali woke up even happier. The whole day he smiled to himself and had joyful and happy thoughts. At supper he ate three times as much as usual and after supper he playfully tapped Allah's knee. "I think, Allah, that you must be very happy that you like me so much. Is it not so? Tell me truly – are you not happy?"

"Very, very happy," answered Allah, smiling.

"I think so too." said Ali. "I know this, my brother

Allah, by myself. Even if I see a dog I like, it makes me happy! But this is only a dog. And this is I! Me, you! I imagine how happy you must be sitting here and looking at me! Your heart must feel warm, is it not so?"

"Warm, very warm," said Allah. "Let's go to sleep."

"Very well! If you wish, let us go to sleep," said Ali.

The next day, Ali walked about deep in thought. At supper he sighed when he looked at Allah, who noticed that once Ali even wiped a furtive tear from his eye. "What is the matter, Ali, why are you so sad?" asked Allah.

"Well, it is about you, Allah, that I am thinking. What would you do without me, Allah? Look how windy and cold it is outside. The rain stings like a whip. What would have happened if you had not found a man you like as well as you like me? Where would you have gone? You would have died of the cold in this wind and rain. You would be soaked to the bone! Here you are where it is warm and dry, you have light, and you have had your supper. How did this come about? It came about because you found a man you liked who would take you in! Without me in the world, you would perish, Allah! It is lucky for you, Allah, that I exist in the world. Truly lucky."

At this Allah could no longer contain himself. He roared with laughter – and vanished. And in his place, on the seat where he had sat, was a pile of large gold coins – two thousand of them.

"O God! What a treasure!" exclaimed Ali's wife wringing her hands. "Is it possible that there could be so much money in the world?"

But Ali pushed her aside and, counting the money, said, "Hmmm ... not much."

Translated by Rowen Glie

Without Allah

Once upon a time, Allah tired of being Allah. He left His throne and His Heaven, and went down to earth as a most ordinary man. He swam in the river, slept on the grass, and for His meal He gathered berries. He went to sleep with the skylarks and woke when the sun tickled His eyelashes.

Life went on as if nothing had happened. Every day the sun would rise and set. In poor weather there was rain. Smiling, Allah looked about and He thought, "The world is like a little stone on a mountain – push it, and it will roll all by itself."

Suddenly a wish came to Allah. He thought, "How do people live without me? The birds are stupid and so are the fish. But how does the clever man do without Allah?" With this in mind, He left the fields, the meadows, and the groves, and went to Baghdad.

"I wonder if the city is still in its place," thought Allah. And indeed the city was exactly where it had always been. The donkeys were making the usual noises and so were the camels. And so were the people. The donkeys were working and so were the camels. And so were the people. Everything was as before: unchanged. "Is My name no more remembered?" wondered Allah.

To discover what people were saying, Allah went to the market. And there He saw a trader selling a horse to a young man. What he witnessed went something like this:

"I swear by Allah," cried the horse trader, this is a young steed! Only three years ago he was weaned from its mother. Ah! What a horse this one is! Mount it and you will become a knight! And this is a horse without faults! In the name of Allah, not one fault, not even a little one."

The young man eyed the horse. "Oh? Is that so?"

The horse trader even twisted his arms and grabbed his turban. "Oh! Stupid! Truly you are a stupid man! How could it be otherwise if I swear to you by Allah? What do you think I am? Do I not care for my own soul?"

The young man bought the horse and paid in gold.

Allah let them finish their transaction and then came closer.

"My good man, why do you swear by Allah when Allah is no more?"

The horse trader was just putting the gold into his purse. He shook the purse, listened to the jingling of gold coins, and snickered, "So what? Would he otherwise buy the horse from me? Now, I can tell you – it was an old horse, and besides, it had a cracked hoof."

Allah smiled and went on his way. Coming toward him was the porter Hussein. The sack he was carrying was bigger than him. Behind Hussein trotted the merchant Ibrahim. Under his heavy load Hussein's feet were wobbly. Sweat was pouring from him like rain. His eyes were bulging. Still Ibrahim walked behind him, nagging and nagging.

"You do not fear Allah, Hussein. You took it on yourself to carry this sack, and you carry it so slowly that we will never be able to transport even three sacks in one day. This is no good, Hussein! No good! You should think about your soul. Allah sees how lazy you are. Allah will punish you, Hussein."

Allah took Ibrahim by the hand and pulled him aside. "Why do you mention Allah? There is no Allah anymore."

Ibrahim scratched his neck. "So I've heard. But what can I do? How else can I make Hussein work faster? The sacks are heavy. But if I give him more money, I will lose. Beat him up? Hussein is stronger than I am. Take him to a judge? He will run away on the way there. But Allah is stronger than any man, and from Allah one cannot run away, so I try to frighten him with Allah."

Allah shook his head and moved on. Anywhere Allah looked, He heard, "Allah" "Allah" "Allah".

The day was drawing to an end. Long shadows started to run from the houses. The sky seemed to be on fire, and from a minaret came the lingering chant of the muezzin, "Lia ill ago ill Allah!"

Allah stopped before the mosque, bowed to the mullah and asked, "Why do you call people to the mosque? There is no Allah anymore."

The frightened mullah got to his feet. "Not so loud! Hush! If you yell, they will hear. Don't you understand? Who will respect me then? Who will even approach me if he learns that Allah is no more?"

Allah frowned and soared up to Heaven like a column of fire before the eyes of the stunned mullah who fell to the ground in fear. Allah returned to His palace and resumed His throne. But He no longer smiled as He looked down upon the earth lying at His feet.

When the first trembling and timid soul of a believer presented itself before Allah, Allah looked at it sternly and asked, "What good did you do on earth?"

"Your name was always on my lips," replied the soul.

Allah shook His head. "What else?"

"Anything I did, I did in the name of Allah," replied the soul. "I also taught others to remember Allah, no matter what my business was or with whom I was doing it. I always told everyone to remember Allah."

"What zeal!" Allah sneered, "And how much money did this zeal bring you?"

The soul started to shake.

"That's just it!" exclaimed Allah and turned away. And Shaitan the devil came on all fours, grabbed the soul by the leg and whisked it away.

Thus did Allah display His anger with the people of the earth!

Translated by Rowen Glie

Truth and Falsehood

A Persian tale

Once a Liar and a man of Truth met on the road near a big city.

"Greetings, Liar," said the Liar.

"Greetings, Liar," answered the man of Truth.

"That's an offence." The Liar was hurt.

"No offence meant. You are a liar indeed."

"That is my life – I always lie."

"And I always tell the truth."

"That's silly." The Liar laughed. "It's not so very impressive to tell the truth. Here is a tree, and so you'll say: here is a tree. Any fool can do that. But in order to invent things you have to use your brain. And in order to use your brain you must have one in the first place. If a man lies, he has a brain. Whereas the man who always tells the truth is a fool – he can't think of anything."

"That's a lie," said the man of Truth. "There's nothing better than the truth. Truth adorns our lives."

"I wonder," sneered the Liar. "Let us go into the city and see who will manage to please people more – you with your truth or I with my falsehood."

"Let's go." And they went.

It was noon and very hot. The streets were deserted. The two men turned into a coffee house. "Greetings, good people!" Some men were languishing under the awning like sleepy flies in the heat.

"It is hot and boring. You have come from afar, so tell us what interesting things you saw during your travels."

"There was nothing of interest," said the man of Truth.

"I just ran into a tiger in the street," said the Liar.

Everybody came alive right away, like wilted flowers sprinkled with water.

"How's that? Where? What sort of tiger?"

"What do you mean 'what sort'? A huge striped beast with bared fangs – like this! And sharp claws – like this! Furiously lashing its sides with its tail. I was all atremble when I saw it from around a corner. Thank Allah it did not notice me or I wouldn't be talking to you now. There's a tiger in the city!"

One of the customers jumped up and shouted to the owner of the coffee house:

"Hey, make me some more coffee. I'll stay here till nightfall. Let my wife shout herself hoarse. How can I go home when there's a tiger prowling about?"

"And I'll go to my rich distant relative Hassan," said another. "He's never keen to see me, but when I tell him about the tiger loose in the city, he's bound to be more hospitable and treat me to some mutton and pilaf, because he'll want to know all about it. We'll feast to the tiger's health."

"And I'll go to the Wali himself," said a third. "He is relaxing at home with his wives – may Allah prolong his days and preserve his wives' beauty – and does not know what is going on in the city. He threatened to imprison me for thievery. But now he'll probably reward me for being the first to tell him the news."

By midday the tiger was the talk of the town. Hundreds of people had seen it with their own eyes.

By evening one man had even been killed by the tiger. It so happened that the Wali's servants caught a thief that day. They beat him up so badly that the poor thief went to perform his evening prayers before Allah's seat in Heaven. The servants became scared, but the next minute they had an idea. They ran to the Wali and said:

"Oh mighty Master! Misfortune! There's a tiger loose in the city and he tore one thief to pieces."

"I know about the tiger, another thief told me. It's not so very impressive that some miserable thief perished. A tiger is bound to eat someone. Thank God it was a thief and not a good person."

After that people crossed to the other side of the street whenever they saw the Wali's servants who, thanks to the tiger, now felt free to beat people to death.

Most people stayed home, and if someone arrived with the news of the tiger he was greeted with honors and treated to the best food.

It was at this point that a young man named Kazim came to the rich Hassan leading his beautiful daughter Rohe by the hand.

Seeing them together Hassan shook with rage.

"How dare you, you wretched beggar, in violation of all rules of decency, bring dishonor upon my family by appearing in public with my daughter, the daughter of the richest man in town?"

"You should thank Allah that your daughter came home at all," said Kazim with a low bow. "The tiger nearly devoured your daughter just now. I was passing the spring where our women go for water and saw your daughter Rohe. Suddenly the tiger jumped out from around a corner. A huge striped beast with bared fangs – like this! Sharp claws out – like this! Furiously lashing its sides with its tail."

"Yes, you must be telling the truth, that is exactly how the tiger was described to me," Hassan whispered, shivering with fear.

"I said to myself: may I perish so that the beautiful Rohe will live. I rushed between the tiger and Rohe with a dagger in my hand. Allah had mercy on me and he preserved my life for something wonderful. And the tiger must have gotten scared: it lashed its sides with its tail, jumped high over a house and disappeared. And I brought your Rohe to you. Forgive me for this."

Hassan clutched his head in anguish:

"Oh woe to me, the old fool that I am! Don't be angry with me, dear Kazim! I should have received you as a guest of honor. Please be seated, dear Kazim, and let me serve you. What can I give you, my courageous warrior, what can I treat you to?"

When Kazim was seated, after numerous bows and entreaties, Hassan turned to his daughter:

"Were you very scared, my little treasure?"

"My heart is still palpitating like that of a wounded bird." Rohe replied.

"How can I reward you, my most fearless young man?" Hassan exclaimed. "Demand what you will of me. Allah is my witness!"

"Allah is among us! He will bear witness," Kazim intoned reverentially. "You are rich, Hassan. But your greatest treasure is your Rohe. You gave her life and you love her. Today I also gave her life and so I have earned the right to love her too. Let us both love her."

Hassan was confused: "Well, I don't know... What will Rohe say?"

Rohe bowed to her father and said: "Allah is a witness to your oath. Do you think your own daughter will make you a perjurer before Allah?"

"Rohe and I have long been in love, but I did not dare ask for her hand. I am poor and you are rich. We used to meet at the spring to lament our fate. That was why I happened to be there today."

Hassan was distressed to hear that: "That's no good!"

"If I had not gone there today, the tiger would have killed your daughter!"

"Let Allah's will be done. We do not move of our own free will, He leads us."

And Hassan gave his blessing to Rohe and Kazim to be married. The whole city praised Kazim for the daring that had earned him a rich and beautiful wife.

Hearing this, the Wali became envious: "I ought to get something out of this tiger too."

So he sent a messenger to Teheran with this letter:

"Grief and joy trade places like day and night. Thank Allah, the dark night that hung over our glorious city is at an end and the sunny day is here again. A fierce tiger attacked our city: a huge striped beast with claws and fangs that were terrible to behold. It jumped over houses and devoured people. Every day my trusted servants reported one or two men eaten by the awful tiger. Everyone lived in terror, but not I. I had decided in my heart: 'I may perish, but I will save the city from the tiger.' Singlehandedly I went to fight the horrible beast. I found it in a deserted alley. The tiger lashed its sides with its tail in fury and then attacked me. However, because I have practiced all the noble skills from a child, I have a fine command of martial arts. I struck the tiger between the eyes with my grandfather's sword and cut its head in two. Thus I delivered the city from the terrible beast. The tiger's skin is being tanned, so it cannot be brought to you any time soon, lest it rot in the heat."

From Teheran came a letter of commendation and a gold-embroidered caftan for the Wali. People were happy for him and he was now the talk of the town.

The man of Truth could no longer tolerate all these lies. He started telling people at crossroads: "Stop repeating lies! There was no tiger. It was invented by the Liar. There is no cause for you to be scared, to boast, and to rejoice. We were walking together and saw no tiger."

"Look at this truthful man! He says there was no tiger!"

When the rumors reached the Wali he summoned the man of Truth before him in great anger. He stamped his feet and shouted: "How dare you spread malicious lies?"

"I'm telling the truth. There was no tiger."

"What is truth? Truth is what the strong and mighty say. When I speak to the Shah, truth is what the Shah says. When I speak to you, truth is what I say. If you want to tell only the truth, buy yourself a slave and whatever you tell him will be the truth. Now tell me this, do you exist?"

"I do," said the man of Truth confidently.

"And I say you don't. I can have you impaled this minute and you will be no more. So I told you the truth – you don't exist. Do you understand?"

But the truthful man insisted: "I will still tell nothing but the truth. There was no tiger. I saw with my own eyes."

The Wali ordered a servant to bring him his gold-embroidered caftan. "What do you see?"

"A golden caftan."

"So now you saw with your own eyes that there was a tiger – if there is this caftan, then there must have been a tiger. Go and tell people the truth. There was a tiger because this golden caftan saw it."

"But the truth…"

"The truth is in your silence. If you want the truth, keep your mouth shut. Go now and remember what I said."

Thus the man of Truth was put to shame. People knew that he was telling the truth, but they kept away from him: who wants to be thought a liar because of repeating his truth? No one wanted anything to do with him.

So he left the city and on the outskirts met the Liar. The Liar looked well-fed, rosy-cheeked, and merry.

"So they chased you away, did they?"

"For once you told the truth," said the man of Truth.

"Now let's compare notes. Which one of us made more people happy? You with your truth or me with my lies? Kazim is happy: he has a rich wife. The Wali is happy: he was given a golden caftan. The townsfolk are all happy not to have been killed by the tiger. The whole city is happy to have such a courageous Wali. And who's behind all this happiness? But whom did you make happy? You are unhappy yourself. No one wants to talk to you. You are chased away from every house. What can you tell them? Only what there is, and what they know only too well without you. Now look at me! I tell them what they don't know because I invent things. People are interested and they want to hear my stories. Yes, you have people's respect but I have the rest: warm welcome and nice food."

"Respect is enough for me," said the man of Truth proudly.

The Liar fairly jumped for joy: "That's a lie! Respect is never enough." The man of Truth blushed and the Liar added: "You also need to eat!"

Translated by Nathalie Roy

The Green Bird

A Persian tale

The Great Vizier Mughabedzin summoned his viziers and said to them:

"The more I observe our governing the more I see how stupid it is."

Everyone froze. No one dared argue.

"What are we doing?" the Great Vizier continued. "We punish evil deeds. What could be more stupid?"

The viziers were amazed but dared not object.

"When a vegetable garden is weeded, the weeds are pulled out with their roots. Whereas we just mow the weeds when we see them and that makes them grow even more thickly. We punish the deeds. But in what are they rooted? In people's minds. We must learn what is going on in those minds if we are to prevent further wrongdoing. Only by knowing what people think can we know who is a good person and who is a bad one, and what to expect from each one. Then we shall be able to punish vices and reward virtues. Meanwhile we are just cutting the grass, but leaving the roots in the ground and letting the grass grow thicker."

The viziers exchanged anxious glances.

"People's thoughts are hidden in their heads," said one, who was braver than the rest. "And since a person's head is a box made of bones, when it cracks the thoughts fly away."

"Human thought is a restless thing and so Allah himself provided it an outlet: the mouth," the Great Vizier countered. "For a person who has a thought to keep it to himself and not divulge it to anyone is unthinkable. We must know people's innermost thoughts, those they share only with those closest to them when they are not afraid of being overheard."

Then the viziers happily exclaimed in chorus:

"We must multiply the number of spies!"

The Great Vizier merely sneered at the idea.

"One man has wealth while another must work. Now take the man who has no wealth and does not work though he eats as well as Allah may grant anyone. Everyone will guess that he is a spy and should be avoided. We have plenty of spies as it is, but all to no avail. To increase their number is to deplete our treasury to no purpose."

The viziers felt perplexed.

"I give you one week to think it over," Mughabedzin announced. "Either you come back in a week and tell me how to read other people's thoughts or you are dismissed. Remember it's a matter of your posts. Go now!"

Six days passed. The viziers merely shrugged when they met.

"Do you have an idea?"

"There is nothing better than spies. Do you have a better idea?"

"Nothing better than spies."

At the court of the Great Vizier there was also a certain young man called Abl-Eddin, a trickster and banterer. He was forever idle, in the sense that he was never doing anything useful. He played all sorts of tricks on honorable people. However, since his victims were people of low rank and his jokes were enjoyed by those of higher rank, Abl-Eddin got away with practically anything. So it was to him that the viziers went for advice.

"Instead of inventing your stupid jokes, why don't you think of something clever for a change?"

"That will be more difficult," said Abl-Eddin and named such a high price that the viziers were impressed:

"Oh, this man has brains."

They pooled their money and after Abl-Eddin received his fee he told them:

"You will be saved. Don't ask me how. It makes no difference to the drowning man how he is pulled out of the water: by the hair or by the hand."

Abl-Eddin went to the Great Vizier and said:

"I am the one who can solve your problem."

Mughabedzin asked: "How?"

"When you order peaches from your gardener, you don't ask him how he means to grow them, right? He will fertilize the peach tree with dung and that will make the peaches sweet. It is the same with the affairs of the state. There is no need for you to know how I am going to do this as long as you get the fruit of my work."

Mughabedzin asked: "What do you need to accomplish your task?"

Abl-Eddin replid: "Just one thing: your permission to do anything I do, no matter how silly it might seem. Even if you fear that you and I could be locked up in a mad house."

To this Mughabedzin retorted:

"I'll remain where I am no matter, but you could be impaled."

Abl-Eddin said: "Let it be as you wish. And one more condition: barley is sown in the autumn but only reaped the following summer. You must give me time: from the next full moon, when I'll sow, till the next full moon, when you'll reap."

"I agree," said Mughabedzin. "But remember: you will pay with your head."

Abl-Eddin laughed at this: "You are going to impale me, but you talk about paying with my head."

He held out a paper to the Great Vizier which he had ready for signature. Having read the paper, the Great Vizier clutched his head in consternation:

"You must be in a hurry to get on the pale!"

But true to his word, he signed the paper. Meanwhile he told the vizier in charge of justice to sharpen a good sturdy pale for the trickster.

The next morning, to the sound of trumpets and drums, the heralds announced the following decree in all the streets and squares of Teheran:

"Residents of Teheran, rejoice! Our most wise Emperor, the Ruler of all rulers, who is brave as a lion and bright as the sun, has put the government of our country in the caring hands of Mughabedzin, may Allah prolong his days to the end of time.

"Mughabedzin has said that in order to make the life of every Persian brighter and merrier, every Persian must keep a parrot in his house as a pet. This bird brings much pleasure to adults and children alike and is a fine adornment to any house. The richest Indian rajahs keep these birds in their houses for entertainment. May every Persian house be adorned the same way as the richest rajah's palace. Moreover, every Persian must remember that the famous 'peacock' throne of the Ruler of rulers, which his ancestors won in the war with the Great Moguls, is decorated with a parrot carved from a single outsize emerald. Therefore, at the sight of this emerald-colored bird every Persian will be reminded of the peacock throne and the Ruler of rulers who sits on it. The solicitous Maghabedzin appoints Abl-Eddin in charge of supplying parrots to our good Persian people who should buy them from him at a set price. This decree must be fulfilled before the new moon.

"Residents of Teheran, rejoice!"

The residents of Teheran were perplexed. The viziers argued quietly among themselves as to who was madder: Abl-Eddin, who wrote the decree, or Mughabedzin, who signed it. Abl-Eddin imported a huge supply of parrots from India, and since he sold them at double the price, he made a tidy profit.

Now a parrot perched in a cage in every house. The vizier in charge of justice sharpened the pale and plated it with tin plates conscientiously.

Abl-Eddin was full of cheer.

The time from one full moon to the next had elapsed. The sparkling moon rose over Teheran. The Great Vizier summoned Abl-Eddin and said:

"Well, my friend, time for you to sit on the pale."

"Perhaps you'll want to give me a more honorable seat," replied Abl-Eddin. "The harvest is ripe, go and reap it. Go and read people's thoughts."

With much pomp, astride a white Arabian steed, accompanied by torch-bearers, Abl-Eddin and all the viziers, Mughabedzin set out to Teheran.

"Where would you like to go first?" Abl-Eddin asked.

"Let it be this house here," the Great Vizier pointed to the nearest house.

The house owner stood rooted to the ground at the sight of such magnificent guests.

The Great Vizier nodded graciously to him and Abl-Eddin said:

"Rejoice, good man! Our solicitous Great Vizier has come to you to find out how you live and whether the green bird gives you joy."

The master of the house bowed and said:

"Since our most wise Lord and Master ordered us to keep this green bird, joy has not left our house. My wife and I, our children and our friends have great fun with the bird. Praise be to the Great Vizier, who brought so much joy to our house."

"Fine, fine!" said Abl-Eddin. "Bring the bird here."

The man brought the cage and put it before the Great Vizier. Abl-Eddin produced some pistachio nuts from his pocket and started pouring them from one hand to the other. Seeing the nuts the parrot tried to reach them. It watched them with one eye and suddenly screamed:

"The Great Vizier is a fool! The Great Vizier is a fool! Fool! Fool!"

The Great Vizier jumped up as though stung. "What a wretched bird!" Enraged he turned to Abl-Eddin: "To the pale with him! This scoundrel must be impaled immediately! How dare you shame me?"

But Abl-Eddin bowed calmly and said:

"This bird could not possibly have thought of this itself. Obviously it heard this said many times in this house. This is what the master of the house says when he thinks that no stranger might overhear. He sings praises to your wisdom to your face, but behind your back..."

Meanwhile the bird, reaching for the nuts, kept screaming: "The Great Vizier is a fool! Abl-Eddin is a thief! Abl-Eddin is a thief!"

"Now you can hear this man's secret thoughts."

The Great Vizier turned to the master of the house: "Is this true?"

The man stood there pale as pale, as if he were already dead.

The parrot went on screaming: "The Great Vizier is a fool!"

"Shut that bloody bird up!" cried Mughabedzin. "And impale the man!"

Abl-Eddin twisted the bird's neck.

Then the Great Vizier said to Abl-Eddin: "Get on my horse. Go on! Now I shall lead it by the bridle. I want all to see that I not only punish people for evil thoughts, but also reward them for wise thoughts."

From then on Mughabedzin, in his own words, "could read other people's minds better than his own."

When he had suspicions about someone, he demanded that their parrot be brought to him. Some pistachio nuts were placed before the parrot and watching them with one eye, the bird blurted out its owner's innermost thoughts: how he cursed the Great Vizier and damned Abl-Eddin. The vizier in charge of justice sharpened one pale after another. Mughabedzin weeded his vegetable garden with such zeal that soon there would be no vegetables left.

Then the most distinguished and wealthy people of Teheran came to Abl-Eddin, bowed to him and said:

"You invented the bird, so you should invent the cat for that bird. What is to be done now?"

Abl-Eddin chuckled and said: "It's not easy to help fools. But if you think of something clever by morning, I'll think of something for you."

The next morning when Abl-Eddin came out into his reception room, the floor was carpeted with banknotes and the merchants bowed to him.

"That's smart of you," said Abl-Eddin. "I'm surprised this simple idea did not enter your heads: you should kill your parrots, buy new ones from me and teach them to say 'Long live the Great Vizier! Abl-Eddin is the benefactor of the Persian people!' That is all you need to do."

The Persians looked with regret at their money strewn all over the floor and left. Meanwhile envy and spite took their toll. Mughabedzin dismissed his numerous spies.

"Why should I feed spies when the people of Teheran feed their own spies right in their homes?" The Great Vizier was amused.

So the former spies, who were left without any means of subsistence, started spreading evil rumors about Abl-Eddin. The rumors reached Mughabedzin.

"All of Teheran is cursing Abl-Eddin and, because of him, the Great Vizier too: 'We have nothing to eat ourselves and now we have to feed these birds.'"

These rumors fell on fertile soil. A government officer is like a meal – when we are hungry we like the smell, and after we have eaten we are nauseated even by its sight. It's the same with government officers. After he has performed his duty he becomes a burden. Mughabedzin eventually tired of Abl-Eddin.

"Haven't I perhaps showered too many distinctions on this upstart? He's become too full of himself. Such a simple idea could easily have come into my own head."

Rumors about people's discontent soon reached Mughabedzin and he summoned Abl-Eddin.

"You did me a bad turn. I hoped you would suggest an effective plan, but you did more harm than good. You let me down. Because of you, people are grumbling and popular discontent is growing. It is your fault. You are a traitor!"

Abl-Eddin bowed and said:

"You can execute me but you should grant me a fair trial. You can impale me, but let us first ask the people if they are really grumbling, if they are really discontent. You have the means to do so. I myself gave you this means. You can turn it against me now."

The next day Mughabedzin, accompanied by Abl-Eddin and all his viziers, rode along the streets of Teheran in order to listen to the voice of the people. The day was hot and sunny and the parrots' cages had been placed on the windowsills. At the sight of the magnificent procession the green birds came to life and screamed:

"Long live the Great Vizier! Abl-Eddin is the benefactor of the Persian people!"

Thus they rode through the whole city.

"These are the Persians' innermost thoughts. This is what they say when they know no one is listening," said Abl-Eddin. "You heard them with your own ears."

Mughabedzin was so moved that his eyes welled with tears. He alighted from his horse, embraced Abl-Eddin and said: "I am guilty before you: I listened to slanderers. I'll have them all impaled. Now get on my horse. I'll lead it through the city by the bridle. Come on! That's an order."

From then on Abl-Eddin remained forever in the Great Vizier's favor.

He was granted a great honor: while he still lived, a beautiful fountain was built in his honor, and inscribed thus: "To Abl-Eddin, benefactor of the Persian people!"

The Great Vizier Mughabedzin lived out his days and died convinced that he had done away with popular discontent and inculcated good intentions in the Persian people.

As for Abl-Eddin, his parrot business thrived and he made huge sums of money. In his diary, from which this story was taken, he wrote: "Thus parrots' voices are often taken for the voice of the people."

Translated by Nathalie Roy

The Portrait of Moses

When Moses led the Jews out of Egypt his fame spread throughout the earth as oil spreads on water. Everyone was amazed by his deed: "A man who can perform such a miracle is surely a saint, one who is agreeable to God."

The fame of Moses reached one of the Arabian kings. The King listened with astonishment to all that Moses had done and then secretly called his best artist-painter and told him, "I would like to see the face of this man of God. Take a tablet made of ivory, your best colors, and go into the desert where Moses is now. With the help of your art, and with the utmost care, make a portrait of Moses and bring it to me. Let this be a secret between you and me. Go!"

The court artist took the ivory tablet, selected his best colors, and left the palace in complete secrecy. He arrived in the desert, found Moses, and made a magnificent portrait which he brought back to the King.

For a long time the King remained before the portrait, looking at the face of the man of God. Then he ordered the portrait to be displayed in the palace and summoned all his sages. His sages had experience in all kinds of secret sciences, and the King often asked them for advice in the affairs of state. The King showed them the portrait, saying, "You, who can read what is hidden like an open scroll, tell me what kind of a man this is and where his strength lies."

The sages studied the portrait at length, then stared at the oldest among them in silence. No one wanted to be the first to express an opinion. They were wisely afraid to be wrong and put to shame. The oldest sage stood before the portrait tugging at his beard. Finally, he said, "This man is mean."

Now the other sages jumped in to lambaste the man in the portrait.

"He is a proud man," said one. "Mean and quick-tempered," added another. "Ambitious!" "Greedy!" "A lover of women!" His face revealed only bad and degrading traits. In chorus, they asserted, "This man is evil. Such a man cannot be agreeable to God!"

"Stop!" The King cried in fury. "What is the matter with you? Do you not know who this is? This is Moses, admired by all the peoples of the world. And you say that he is not agreeable to God! Everyone is amazed by his virtues and you find in him only defects. Now do I see the value of your wisdom!" The King tore his clothes in a sign of sorrow. "Pity me for listening to you on affairs of state!"

The frightened sages fell to their knees, and the oldest of them said, "Our science is true. And what we say is the truth. The artist must be guilty! He did not draw the face of this great man correctly and so confused us. Order his execution!"

Now an argument started.

The artist said, "I painted his face correctly, it is you sages who have erred."

The sages persisted, "The artist did a poor job."

The King wanted to find the truth by any and all means. He ordered his chariot and drove out into the desert. There, raising his eyes, he saw from afar a man whose face resembled the face in the portrait as one pea resembles another in a pod. "Who is this?" the King asked.

"God's man, Moses," they answered.

The King came closer, produced the portrait and compared the face in the picture with the face of Moses. He found that Moses was represented by the artist with perfect art and resemblance, and that the face of Moses in the painting seemed alive. The King, bewildered and amazed, said that he wanted to talk to Moses.

Coming into Moses' tent, the King made a low bow to the man of God and told him about the dispute between the artist and the sages.

"Forgive me, man of God! Until I saw your face I thought that the artist was wrong and had not created a true likeness of you, because my sages are the wisest in the world and know perfectly their sciences. But now, when I see that the living you and the painted you are as alike as two peas, I know the value of their wisdom. They lied to me. But, still they ate my bread and made a fool of me with their nonsense."

Moses smiled, and answered, "No! Both the artist and your sages are truly remarkable specialists in their arts. But you must know that if I were what people think I am, judging by my actions, I would be no better than a dry log without one human defect. I would have no merit before God or before people. I am not ashamed to tell you that all the defects which your sages discovered in me are indeed inherent in me, maybe even to a greater degree than your sages thought. But I have conquered all my bad passions. As one grows a tree from a seed, I grew good in me. I accustomed myself to doing good until doing good became second nature. This is why I am liked in Heaven as well as on earth."

Thus, with a kind smile, Moses let the Arabian King go home in peace.

Translated by Rowen Glie

The Birth of Jesus

A Moslem Tale

"There is no God but God the Unique, and Jesus is His prophet!" So said the All-Powerful, whose glory imparts the redolence of the universe and whose fame grows like flowers on the earth.

"Peace and joy to my earth! Peace and joy to my

people! My earth is filled with piety and the hearts of men are filled with faith in me. Smoke soars over the earth carrying prayers and incense to my throne. The earth shines with precious temples; for my glory do they erect the precious temples, to glorify my name in them. Joy and peace to my beloved earth! Joy and peace to my beloved people!" So said the Judge of Heaven and earth.

"But I am neither in temples nor in battles. I am in love. Their hearts are filled with love and piety for me, but they do not have love for one another. Blessed be the earth and the peoples on it. Peace and love shall grow on the earth. I will send to them a prophet. Let him reveal to them my commandments." So Allah spoke, and His breath was like the breath of spring.

On a white horse there appeared before Him the Knight of Knights, Gabriel, the beloved messenger of Allah. He came on his winged white horse and the seraphs joyfully shook their white wings amidst a snowy field. And it was with rapture that he listened to the word of God the Unique whose name shall be glorified forever and ever! "Go forth on the earth and from Heavenly fire kindle love for men in the heart of a newborn baby. Let him bring to humanity peace and love." So said the Omnipotent, and His breath lighted Gabriel's torch.

Gabriel descended to the palace of the most powerful king on the earth. There, the queen had just brought into the world a male child. They took the newborn and put him on the throne. Before him warriors kneeled; people bowed to him and swore their allegiance to the king's first born.

Gabriel said to the king, "Peace and joy to you! Your son is chosen by Allah. Through him peace and love will reign on the earth. I will kindle in his heart a Heavenly fire. He will be meek and he will be love. He will forgive his enemies. He will not avenge their insults and he will never take up a sword."

The king fell to the ground before God's messenger, tore his clothes in a sign of mourning.

"Woe unto me! Woe for what I did to make Allah angry. Why should I be the father of a coward? Shall the son of a powerful king kiss the hand of his enemy? Will he swallow offenses as the lowest of slaves? A son who will never hold a sword in his hand? It would be better if he would not be born. It would be better if his mother would shame me by remaining childless. Oh, it would be better for me to be dead before his conception than to see with my own eyes such a disgrace. Messenger of God! Let such a great wrath of God be avoided. Have pity! Take your flaming torch away from my house."

The sorrowful archangel flew away and knocked at the door of a very rich man. The fame of this rich man was greater than that of kings. His caravans travelled throughout the world and his ships sailed on all seas, bringing to all corners of the world uncountable treasures. He had everything. For only one thing did he piously pray to Allah: he longed for a son, an heir to his fortune. And a son was born to him. At this happy moment the messenger of God stood before the richest man in the world.

"Happiness and joy to you. Happiness not expressible in words is visiting you. Thy son is chosen by Allah. His name will be love. He will appease tears and sorrow. He will give his riches to the poor. He will walk in the world like the poorest of men, happy and joyful with his love for the people."

The rich man prostrated himself before the messenger of God, and tearing from himself his precious jewels, he started to wail.

"O, woe to me! Why was I so cursed? In punishment for my greediness does Allah kill me! For what did I gather my immense riches? My son will be a beggar! He will give away all that his father amassed. What greater punishment could there be for a rich man than to have a spender for a son? What sacrifices shall I bring to Allah to have pity on me and prevent the ruin of my house? What temples should I erect so that, seeing my piety, He would pity me and not destroy my child?"

So sobbed the rich man, and the archangel felt pity for him and flew away.

On this cold winter night Gabriel descended like an eagle into a cave where the wind howled and a young mother was bending over a baby dying of cold. She gave birth to him here, having no place to go. The archangel had pity for the dying child, and to give him some warmth, touched him with the flaming torch.

The baby smiled. From his smile the stars started to smile, and in horror Gabriel declared, "What did I do with the fire of Allah? In what feeble hands did I put the gift of Allah?"

The young mother prostrated herself and said, "Amen to the wish of God!"

Gabriel stood in terror. Then the voice and laughter of Allah reached his ears. From joy Allah laughed, and so did the stars, the moon, and the baby.

"Gabriel, Gabriel! How do you fulfill my will? Are there kings for the Omnipotent? Are there rich men for me when everything belongs to me anyway? Are there powerful people before the All-Powerful? Is not everyone equal before me? And who are my kings? My kings are in rags. My kings are in temples and market places, in dust, in ashes. Covered by wounds are my kings. My kings are tremendously rich as they have the most precious gifts. Their tears are diamonds, and rubies are their hearts. Out of their hearts I weave a crown for myself; with their tears I adorn my mantle. My kings are powerful. Their curse is an order to me — their order I fulfill. Their words are steel swords, and their glances have more power than arrows. Their armies are uncountable — the homeless and the sick, while all angels serve them as shields. I like my kings and I am their Sovereign. I am the God of the poor."

So said Allah with carefree laughter, a laughter of happiness, and the stars laughed with Him, shining to the homeless beggars.

Happy after these words and the smile of the child, the archangel Gabriel soared like an eagle, his torch shining among the stars like a new star.

Kings and rich men came and bowed to the king born on a cold night in a cave.

There is no God but God the Unique, and Jesus is His prophet.

Translated by Rowen Glie

The Legend of the Invention of Gunpowder

The cloister slept.
Only in the cell of Father Bertold a light glimmered. Father Bertold always worked at night. Very often the morning light found him behind flasks and retorts engrossed in his usual strange and mysterious work. Then Father Bertold would make the sign of the cross and go to day-long

prayers so as to continue his work in the evening using his peculiar instruments. Father Bertold would allow himself two or three hours of sleep to sustain his sinful flesh. Pray by day, work by night. Father Bertold mortified his flesh. He had the look of a dried-out ascetic, with parchment skin stretched tight over his body: a dead man to whom anything worldly is foreign. Only his eyes were alive, ablaze with the fanatical fire that burned in his brain.

"He is either a great sinner or a great saint," they said in the monastery, but even the prior never tried to discover the nature of the mysterious work with which Father Bertold was so busy. He only asked, "Is your work for the glory of our great church?"

"Oh, yes," said the monk, and a fanatical flame flashed like lightning in his eyes. "If God will help me, happiness and peace will reign among men. They will give themselves to the Only One God, and the enemies of our holy church will be crushed forever."

"Let God bless your work and strengthen your faith," said the prior.

"Amen!" replied the monk, and there was in his voice such a strong, sincere, and fiery faith that the prior had no more doubts.

Father Bertold was truly occupying himself with a task agreeable to God and useful to the holy church.

Thereafter Father Bertold was able to work at night unhindered. But on this night, he was not busy with his flasks and retorts. With fiery eyes he remained at the high trellised window that separated the cloister from the sinful world. He remained there with his hot face touching the trellis. Father Bertold looked up at the dark sky studded with stars, down at the valley sunk in darkness, and on the sleeping city visible from the cloister's hill. In his soul, Father Bertold felt a vague anxiety which for several days had kept him from his prayers and his work. This was the devil tempting him and filling his soul with a strange dread, so as to hinder Father Bertold in his great and holy task.

With this indefinable anxiety in his soul, Father Bertold was unable to go back to his great work – the invention of man-made gold. "Yes, this will cut off the head of the serpent," thought Father Bertold. "This will deprive the devil of the weapon with which he conquers the world and fights the holy church. These sparkling particles that the devil uses to blind the minds of men will be produced in ordinary workshops by ordinary craftsmen. Gold will not be valued more than clay. No more will it be a rarity! Humanity will have gold any time it wishes and as much as it wishes, in surplus. It will no longer be the sovereign of the world. Rich men will be no more. Equality will reign among men. There will be no need to tire one's self with hard work. There will be nothing for which to strive, to fight, to have, or to envy. All men will become brothers and will serve the Only One God, and no one else, because people exist to do good, but the devil confuses them with golden nets."

But why had doubts suddenly squeezed into the soul of Father Bertold? What was the doubt that hindered the good father and prevented him from continuing his great work of saving the world from the power of the devil? His great work had made good progress. Already in the oven small golden grains were shining. "This is not yet true gold, just the first image of it, an embryo of gold," thought Father Bertold. "The particles already have many common points with gold. Some more effort and these dust particles will surely transform themselves into pure gold which anyone can prepare for himself in any amount. The power of the devil will be at an end."

And just then, when Father Bertold needed all his faith, a doubt crept into his soul. A wolf eats a calf, a spider devours a fly, and man devours a man. And the old adage, Homo homini lupus est, presses on his brain like lead: "Man is to man a wolf."

In the wrinkled faces of the pilgrims who came to the cloister with tales of battle, Father Bertold read the hate, spite, and cruelty that reigned the world over. "Did not Cain kill Abel before anyone knew about gold, this cursed and contemptuous metal?" he thought. Even in the gospels Father Bertold read about man's meanness, hatred, and cruelty. "Meanness and hate rule the earth, and our holy church tries to teach men goodness and love – to train a vulture to eat grains of wheat and a wolf to eat grass." Even from the autos-da-fé of the Inquisition, there came to Father Bertold the smell of the fires of hatred and cruelty. The smoke from those fires seemed to him a shock of hate that spread over the whole earth.

In vain, Father Bertold knelt before a holy crucifix and stared for hours at the face of the one crucified, seeking consolation and succor for his sorrow. There on the ground, at the base of the cross, he could see the faces of men in whose eyes shone spite, hate, and cruelty. Unappeasable hate, centuries old, has ruled the hearts of men from the very creation of the world.

The warm, silent night descended upon the earth, bringing with it peace, rest, and beneficial sleep. But to Father Bertold it seemed that it was not a salutary night, not a messenger of Heaven, but a monster that was crawling over the earth, hiding with its dark cloak richly decorated with gold everyone afraid of the daylight. "How many crimes are committed under the cover of night?" he mused. "All emotions fall asleep except human hate, which knows no day and no night, no sleep, no rest, no peace. In this very city, right now, people are plotting crimes, lying in wait to ambush and kill." Father Bertold seemed to feel on his own face the breathing of centuries-old hatred filling the air of the whole world.

In his heart a doubt was born: "Is it true that men are created for good and love?" He knew what this meant: the devil was tempting him as he had tempted St. Dionysius. He had read about it in the annals.

St. Dionysius was a great ascetic and the devil was anxious to push him off the path of virtue, humility, and asceticism. The eyes of St. Dionysius were always fixed on the earth because the earth is the beginning and the end of human life. Even going to church, he would watch his step so as not hurt any little creature by accident. If he saw a beetle in his path, he would carefully pick it up and remove it to a safe place far from passersby so that no one would unwillingly hurt this tiny creation of God. Every one of his good deeds was a great shame to the devil, since there is no greater disgrace for the devil than the good deed of a man. Because of St. Dionysius, the devil was exposed to shame and disgrace.

Thus, the devil began to tempt St. Dionysius. The devil came to him dressed as an Eastern ambassador. He brought sumptuous treasures and invited the saint to a supposed kingdom where he might make thousands of people happy and acquire world-wide glory for himself. The saint, however, was not lured by wealth, glory, and power, and did not cease to serve the Only One God.

St. Dionysius used to fast and when he was weak from hunger, the devil would put before him rich tables laden with the fine food, aromatic drinks, and exotic ripe fruit. St. Dionysius would look on all this and continue his fast, putting the devil to shame.

When St. Dionysius was working and suffering from the heat of the day, cool forests would suddenly grow up before him, forests in which murmured crystal clear brooks and where marvelous birds sang. The trees would silently wave their branches and would try to lure the saint to rest during the hour fixed for prayers. But St. Dionysius would kneel and pray even longer, even if burned by the rays of the summer sun.

Then the devil, put to shame so many times, decided to frighten St. Dionysius with holy fear, and appeared before the saint in all his Satanic glory. But St. Dionysius, who was innocent before God, felt no fear in his pure heart. Without trembling, he looked at the devil and even described his appearance in the annals. "His eyes were as coals, his breath like sulfur, and the look in his eyes was as burning saltpeter," wrote St. Dionysius.

"Sulfur, saltpeter, and coal... sulfur, saltpeter, and coal... this is the formula of the tempter," murmured Father Bertold.

With firm steps, Father Bertold went to the oven. He had decided to call on the devil and look straight into his Satanic face. Like St. Dionysius, he would put the devil to shame.

Returning to his laboratory, he mixed sulfur, coal, and saltpeter in a mortar, raised high his pestle, and brought it down with great force on the mortar. "Incubus! Incubus! Incubus!" he incanted.

A terrifying roar shook the cloister to its foundations. A column of fire soared from the mortar and amidst the fire appeared someone with a Satanic smile and a golden sword in hand. "Thank you, friend," he said with a voice that made Father Bertold's heart turn to ice and stop beating. "You helped me come out of this mixture. You rendered me a great service. From now on people will not have to kill each other only one by one, face to face. Now they will be able to kill from afar and destroy entire cities. You did me a favor. You put a sword in the hand of the insane and created a perfect weapon for human hatred." With that, he vanished, filling the air with smoke and a foul stench.

When the frightened monks, led by the prior, rushed into Father Bertold's cell they found him on the floor, as still as a corpse. "He saw the devil," said the prior, who knew what he was talking about, "and the devil burned his face with hellfire. Look at these black points which are imbedded in his face and hands. So often, the striving for knowledge brings us to sin. Good intentions make for a bad end. With knowledge comes doubt, and to doubt is a sin. Fear knowledge, my children!"

The monks listened with fear and confusion gripping their hearts. They sprinkled holy water on Father Bertold. Little by little he recovered, opened his eyes, and terror was in them. "What are you murmuring?" asked the prior. "What prayer are you saying?"

"Sulfur, saltpeter, and coal." Like a madman, Father Bertold kept repeating: "Sulfur, saltpeter, and coal..."

"Sulfur, saltpeter, and coal." The awestruck monks repeated after him.

"I forbid you, in the name of the church, to repeat this formula of the tempter. Temptation must not be introduced into the world," said the prior solemnly, and the monks replied, "Amen!"

But the formula was already spoken. In fright, the monks repeated it among themselves and talked of the strange adventure that had befallen Father Bertold. Overheard by laypeople, the tempter's terrible formula flew round the world: sulfur, saltpeter, and coal.

Not one layman saw the black face of Father Bertold.

He immured himself alive into an underground cell and begged the prior to say for him the prayer for the dead. Day and night he asked God to forgive his unforgivable sin. Now the world was completely foreign to him, and he to the world. Only rarely would the monk who brought Father Bertold a little bread and water every week tell him about the terrible disasters, the blood-soaked fields, the razed towns, and other outrages committed by people with the help of sulfur, saltpeter, and coal.

Father Bertold, in deadly terror, would prostrate himself on the floor of his cell. "Will I ever atone for my terrible sin?" he would cry. And before his eyes, in the darkness of the cell-tomb, would appear an apparition with a Satanic smile on his face and a golden sword in his hands, saying, "You rendered me a great service, friend."

And Father Bertold's heart would freeze and stop.

Translated by Rowen Glie

Indian Tales

Statistics

An Indian Legend

The Heavens shook with thunder. Magadewa was terrifying in his righteous anger. The lightning-flashes of his glances burnt into the Heavens, and in the scorched spots new stars flared up, casting a baleful gaze upon the earth.

"Monstrous world of deceit and lies!" thundered Magadewa. And his voice was as the roaring waters of the Deluge. "Miserable clump of mud! My botched attempt! The stench of falsehood rises up from you to the very Heavens! I know of no truth or justice to be found on this wretched earth."

In fury Magadewa smote his Heavens with his rod. And from the gaping rent there appeared before him a new goddess, timid, trembling and beautiful. Her name was Statistics.

"What is the desire of the god of gods, the master of Heaven and earth?" she asked, kneeling before him.

"The gods have been spoilt with sacrifices!" cried Magadewa. "You are uncorrupted. I have just created you. Descend to earth, learn all there is to learn, then return and tell me what is happening there!"

The goddess slid through the clouds and down a rainbow to arrive on earth. She found herself in the holy city of Kendi.

"It's really not at all bad here on earth," she said with a smile as she looked around her.

Her joyful smile was returned with the gloomy one of a young man walking toward her. He was a fakir, devoted to mortification of the flesh and sublime thoughts about things to be found no lower than the ninth Heaven. He was somewhat hirsute in appearance, but not at all bad-looking. The goddess took a liking to him and went after him.

"So, let us occupy ourselves with sublime thoughts!" said the fakir when the goddess followed him into his hut. They talked about much of what is to be found in the ninth Heaven. So much indeed that they themselves were swept up to the ninth Heaven.

When it was time for lunch, the fakir took eight grains of rice from a tiny bag, set four before the goddess and four before himself and said: "If you please!"

"Oh dear!" thought the goddess. "But I am really hungry!" And since she was the goddess Statistics, she started doing some calculations.

"How many grains of rice do you eat a day, my little reed?"

"Eight, my little palm."

She tried to divide eight by three, but it wouldn't go.

"That's no good," she told herself. "Suppose we keep ascending to the ninth Heaven like this and end up one day with three of us... This math leads to no good!"

And since the goddess was a woman, she decided: "No, I'll have to leave this long-haired fakir. You can't live it up on eight grains of rice!"

She ate her four grains, and when the fakir had gone to bed she set off to roam the streets, wondering if she might find somewhere to eat.

Suddenly there appeared from out of nowhere a young man with an unusually white face.

"Such a pretty young miss, and all alone!" he said with

a smile by no means as gloomy as that of the long-haired fakir.

"I'm not a miss, I'm a goddess."

"Be my goddess! I've no objection to that!"

"My name is Statistics."

"And mine's John. Just call me Johnny. Dear Johnny, darling Johnny – whatever you like! I'm one of the English civil servants sent here to run the country, one of the people in charge. But for you I am the humblest of servants. Will you have some ginger beer and a sandwich?"

Deftly bending one arm, he offered this food to the famished goddess.

She found the sandwich delicious, as it looked like a pretzel.

Sitting in the restaurant with Johnny the goddess thought to herself, "This tow haired fellow is much better than any long-haired fakir!" Out loud she said, "I'd like to come to this nice place with you more often."

"Every day if you like!"

And Johnny gave her such a smacker of a kiss that it made her ears ring.

"Hey, Johnny, well done!" said his colleagues at work. "That's quite some charmer you've taken up with!"

Johnny was a happy-go-lucky, goodhearted chap. "Would you like to meet her?" he asked.

"What's her name?"

"These Indians always have such strange names. Statistics – can you imagine that?"

That evening he arrived at the restaurant in the company of his colleagues.

"Goddess!" he said. "These English civil servants have all come to pay their respects."

Statistics counted eight of them. Thirty bottles of ginger beer were consumed.

"My dear," she said to Johnny, now on his sixth bottle, "aren't you drinking too much?"

"Stuff and nonsense! Thirty bottles, ten people. That's three bottles a head. Same again!"

Statistics found this highly amusing. The following evening they met again for supper. After drinking eight bottles on his own, Johnny said: "Thirty bottles, ten people. That's three each. Same again!"

These suppers continued every evening. Downing his fifth bottle, Johnny would shout: "Statistics! How much have I drunk?"

Her merry, full-throated laughter rang out like the songs of hundreds of songbirds as she calculated: "Twenty bottles, ten people. So you've drunk two!"

They had such fun, and Statistics learnt to calculate remarkably quickly. But then one midnight hour when the whole world was asleep under the watchful gaze of the stars, the goddess heard the voice of Magadewa summoning her to his presence. She appeared before him bejewelled and rouged, decked out in all her finery.

"You've become quite a beauty down there on earth!" said Magadewa approvingly.

"It's very pleasant on earth," she said, bowing.

"Did you study the earth as I commanded?"

"Yes, O Master!"

"We shall find out!" said Magadewa, pointing to the earth. 'Do you see that little speck moving down there?"

"Yes, it's a coolie taking a gentleman somewhere in his rickshaw after a late-night spree."

"Poor coolie! I'd like to know what sort of a life he lives and what he has to call his own."

"One moment!" said the goddess, and she started working this out in her head. Now, she thought, the gentleman has a hundred pounds left in his pocket after his night out. And the coolie has twopence. That's a total of a hundred pounds and two pence between the two of them. So that means for each of them there's...

"I have it, O Father of the Gods!'

"Well?"

"The coolie's share is fifty pounds and one penny."

"Aha!' exclaimed Magadewa approvingly. "In their cities even the poor live well. Let's see how it is in the countryside. In the middle of that palm forest, on the shores of a tranquil lake, stands a moonlit village. Tell me how many working elephants there are for each villager."

Statistics began her mental arithmetic. A hundred villagers, one of whom owned a hundred and twenty elephants. He'd bought up the whole herd cheap when everyone was destitute, and now he hired them out to work at a stiff price. So all in all a hundred and twenty elephants and a hundred villagers. Dividing one into the other came to... came to...

"For each person there is more than one elephant!" exclaimed Statistics.

"By the sacred name of Nirvana!" exclaimed Magadewa. "That is more than admirable. But then why are the inhabitants of this planet always complaining? I can't understand it!"

And affectionately he patted the cheek of the goddess, who had acquired such beauty on earth.

"Tell me though," he asked her, "how did you learn to calculate so quickly and with such accuracy?"

"I was taught to do so by English civil servants," replied Statistics.

"Well, hats off to those English civil servants!" said Magadewa.

The goddess beamed with pleasure.

Translated by John Dewey

Reform

A Hindu Legend

This legend was told to the author by "a fakir who had not opened his mouth for thirty years but broke his vow of silence for the author." May Brahma, Vishnu, Siva, and all the Indian deities bless him.

She was born on the shore of the sacred River Ganges with the first ray of the sun on the first morning of Spring — the Goddess Reforma, the beautiful and graceful, with a most supple body. Nature did not spare colors in adorning her, and granted her coal-like black eyes and a lovely pinkish skin. Her hair seemed to be woven of pure sunrays. She was dressed in colors only: she came naked, exquisitely beautiful, free and bold in her movements.

Nature created her in a moment of inspiration. Seeing the goddess, the sun poured brighter and stronger golden rays on the earth. The earth smiled to her with flowers. Seeing her, the palms pensively shook their heads and gently whispered to one another, "How exquisite she is! How lovely!" A gazelle looked at her through the thickets of lianas, and the eyes of gazelles have been beautiful ever since. Seeing her, the tigers, captivated by the beauty of the newborn goddess, purred and stretched their graceful bodies so that she would pet them. Snakes slithered at her feet but would not hurt her. The first people to notice her were the shepherds, the very shepherds who grazed their flocks on a barren, sun-seared mountain. As hungry and tired as they were, they could not contain their cries of delight. The sight of her made them forget all past sorrows and sufferings.

When the goddess appeared on the horizon it seemed that she had just descended from the sky and was flying in the air, hardly touching the flowers with her graceful feet. The shepherds prostrated themselves before her and in their ravishment, could not tear their eyes from her, following her as if hypnotized. The goddess brought them and their flocks to a luxuriant, fertile, blooming field, left them there, and then went to the sacred city of Delhi.

In Delhi, the first to notice her were the Hindu youths. Immediately their hearts beat with a burning and passionate love for the beautiful goddess. Following after the youths came the women, and after the women came their husbands. The old people and the very young ones all fell in love with the goddess and followed her, repeating, "How lovely she is! How lovely!"

Indeed! She was born on the first spring day with the first ray of the springtime sun. The air, warm, tender, gentle, and filled with the scent of flowers, seemed to be her breath. And her breath made everyone around breathe deeply with her. The weather turned hot, and seeking some coolness, she entered the ancient temple of Trimurti.

Inside the temple it was as dark and cold as in a damp cellar, and it smelled of mold and rot. The huge embrasures of the windows were tightly locked. When the doors opened, a shy ray of light would penetrate the heavy darkness, and before it melted in the gloomy dusk something gleamed and sparkled in the depth of the temple. What was it that sparkled there? A raised sword, held over people's heads? A lance directed at the breasts of praying people? Arrows ready to fly from the bow and bring bloodshed and death? No one knew!

In this darkness, the trembling and frightened people clutched at the wide-hemmed clothes of the old Brahmins and begged, "Pray for us to the terrible divinity which blinks at us from the depths of the temple."

Before the divinity, on the altar, were heaps of lotuses left from the preceding year. They were filling the temple with the stench of decay and mold. The Brahmins were singing a chant which would have been appropriate to sing when the lotuses were fresh and full of scent. "It is by your mercy that we inhale the scent of these newly bloomed lotuses that have been brought to you in sacrifice. In the same way as do our prayers, may this pure and fine scent rise to your throne, O Divinity, and may your heart be filled with it." Everyone inhaled the stench of putrefaction and sang about the scent. No one understood anything, but this fact only increased their piety.

On entering the temple, the goddess exclaimed, "Open the windows! Open the windows! Open them now!" The crowd, attentive to every one of her words, hastened to unlatch the huge windows. Waves of light, hot and bright, rushed in and filled the temple, and the people, in wild rapture, for the first time in their lives were able to see the gold divinity standing in the depths of the temple. There were no threateningly raised swords, nor pitilessly directed lances, nor arrows set on taught bows ready to fly away and wreak havoc and death. The divinity did not want to kill anybody. He looked back at the people with a tender smile on each of his three faces. "Throw out these rotten flowers," said the goddess, "And replace them with fresh flowers from the fields."

"But the divinity needs lotuses!" the Brahmins tried to argue.

"The divinity needs the scent of fresh-cut flowers," said the goddess, "Flowers! Flowers here! Flowers from the fields, adorned with the diamonds of dew!" The crowd rushed to obey the goddess's command. The rotten heaps of old lotuses were thrown out. The altar was now piled high with fresh-cut, sweet-smelling flowers still covered with dew. People, young and old, women and children carried bunches of flowers to the temple. They scattered them along the road and on this carpet of flowers more people bravely came to see the gentle and kind divinity with three smiles.

The priests were forgotten. No one asked them for help or for protection any more. Everyone went to the gods by themselves. The women raised their children to the divinity, asking the kind Trimurti for blessings. With eyes full of wonder, the old people looked at the smiling god. "And we thought he was bloodthirsty!" they said. They crowded near the divinity, pushing one another and trying to touch his golden clothes. Trimurti, kind and smiling with three smiles on his three faces, showered on them his triple blessings and joy.

After resting in the temple, the goddess, full of energy and joy, went out onto the main street of Delhi, followed by a huge crowd of people. On the central square rose a newly prepared pyre of aromatic trees. On the pyre, under a white blanket, lay the emaciated body of the old Raja who had recently died. The dead Raja's young and beautiful widow, dressed in her best sari, with tears in her eyes, was ready to join her husband on the pyre. But, at this very moment, the good and joyful goddess approached her. "You wish to die? And why not?" asked the goddess merrily. "Is not life only a gift given by Heaven to people? If you want to refuse the gift, do so! You want to give your body to fire? Give it! Your body is yours! But why do you wish to give to fire your fine clothes? The Raja needs you, your body, but not your clothes. The Raja does not need clothes. He it is who used to remove your clothes from your body. Give yourself to the Raja as you used to. Take your clothes off! Why make the fire take your clothes off? Let the Raja immediately cover your body with kisses – and give the clothes to the poor. That will make one more good deed before you die. Why are you crying?"

"I am afraid to die," the Raja's widow sobbed.

"Why then do you wish to die?" asked the goddess.

"It is required by law, custom, and the people," said the widow. "People want the sacred law to be obeyed."

"Obey it! But before you do, perform a good deed. Take off your clothes!" said the goddess. "Let the poor people take them and they will bless the memory of you and your husband."

The young woman obeyed the goddess, removing her clothes and giving them to the people standing nearby. "Take them!" she said.

The sight of her standing there naked and beautiful sent a whisper of admiration through the crowd. "How lovely she is! Almost as beautiful as the goddess!" Their hearts filled with pity, and many cried out, "Do not do it! Do not die! Do not! She shall not step onto the pyre!"

The goddess smiled at a young man who was staring at her with passion and admiration. "You are in love with me! But I was born in Heaven and everything that is earthly is alien to me. Now look at this woman. Is she not as lovely as I am? Doesn't beauty flood the earth as well as Heaven? Beauty is the sky. Your life is the water. The sky is reflected in the water and that is why water seems to be blue. Look how beautiful she is. Take her and you will have in her my reflection on the earth. Take her!"

The young man glanced at the Raja's naked widow, and his eyes flashed with passion. And the goddess said to the widow, "You want to die in fire? Fire fills our hearts, too. This young man will also put you to fire with his flame. He will clasp you in his arms, and embrace you in his fire. And more than once will you die. Day and night you will feel your soul separate from your body. Immolate yourself in this way!"

The young woman, pink from confusion and passion, threw the torch onto the sweet-smelling pyre on which lay the long, lonely, and emaciated body of the old Raja, and reaching for the young man, she said to him, "Cover me with your cloak and take me away from here."

That year the heat was terrible. The god Indra – in anger, so the Brahmins said – was pitilessly and cruelly searing the earth with blazing rays of sun. The fields stood black, as if charred, and people, thin as skeletons and dying from hunger, came to the city and collapsed on the streets, saying, "Unless you give us food, we will die right here and the stench of our dead bodies will poison the air."

The Brahmins decided to take the statue of Indra out of the temple and carry it around the city. The cruel god was conveyed on a tremendous carriage pulled by ten huge black elephants. Hundreds of people threw themselves under the elephants' feet or under the wheels of the carriage and were crushed, writhing in terrible pain as they died. Before dying, they cried, "The god Indra does not hear the quiet moaning of the sufferers. Let him hear our screams, and let him be terrified by the sight of our ruin. Maybe he will relent and his anger will give way to pity."

The procession was moving slowly through screams,

wails, and moans meant to make the divinity notice the human suffering. The elephants, their feet covered with human blood, continued to crush people lying on the roads as the huge wheels, red and wet, sank into piles of shattered bodies. The procession moved pitilessly on.

The goddess went out to face the procession. Under the rays of the setting sun, she was so beautiful that the elephant drivers brought their black elephants to a dead stop. Looking at the goddess with eyes filled with delight, they were unable to go on. The goddess stood in their way. They could not drive the procession over that wondrously beautiful woman. They turned back the elephants, and the bloody parade returned to the dreary temple of Indra, stepping over corpses that were already stiffening. The ones who lay ahead of the procession, waiting for death, were thereby saved.

Thus the goddess passed her first day on earth.

Next morning, with the sun's first rays, the Brahmins gathered in council. "Because of this new goddess, the faith in the old gods will perish," said one.

"We will all perish!" said another. "No one needs our prayers! They will all pray for themselves."

"She spreads dishonor!" said still another. "Widows no longer want to die to remain true to their husbands."

"She will bring on us the ire of Indra; he will be deprived of sacrifices!" said another. So they sat, thinking hard about what to do.

"Kill her!" said someone timidly. The suggestion was not even dignified with an answer – how could one kill an immortal goddess?

Then the eldest and wisest of the Brahmins rose. "We will imprison her in a cave. We will tell the people that the goddess has flown back up to Heaven. In her absence, people will return to piety. Let her stay in the cave. Later, we can even let her out. By that time she will be old and ugly and no one will lose his head because of her."

Everyone approved of this advice and they prostrated themselves before the eldest Brahmin: "Your advice is a good, time-tested remedy!"

Armed with swords and lances, they went to the spring where the goddess slept on a bed of flowers at night. They surrounded her and came out of hiding, forming a close ring. But the goddess, upon seeing them, joyfully called out, "Come to me! Come to me!" Local residents, on hearing her merry resounding voice, came rushing: they wanted to know what new joy had come into the head of the awakened goddess.

The Brahmins, seeing themselves surrounded, did not dare touch the goddess. They bowed low and said, "We have come to prostrate ourselves before you, and we have brought arms in order to honor you as a sovereign." Then they laid their arms at her feet as a sign of submission.

The Brahmins became completely despondent. "We have to save ourselves and the people from the wrath of Indra and other gods," they said, and so they held another meeting.

For three days and three nights they conferred and thought about what to do. On the fourth day, satisfied and joyful, they came out of the temple and addressed the first passing worshippers of the new goddess. "You all worship the new goddess," they said, "and so do we, because she is divinely beautiful. But you do not care about her at all. The goddess walks naked. The wind touches her and so do the sun's rays. The sun will parch her skin and the wind will make it rough. It is time for you to think about some clothes for the goddess, so that she keeps her beauty, and so that her clothes give her the majestic appearance becoming to her. Adorn her! Show her your love."

"How true!" exclaimed the goddess's worshippers.

"How is it that we did not think of that a long time ago?" They expressed their gratitude to the Brahmins for this wonderful idea and ran to share it with their friends. The Brahmins repeated it to everyone they met, and everyone, finding the idea wonderful, thanked them for it.

Then the people gathered around the goddess to discuss the question, "What is the proper dress for a goddess?" Some said, "There are stuffs as gossamer as a spider's web, hardly visible. We will get these stuffs and we will make a dress for the goddess so that not one line of her divine body will be lost to the eyes!"

Others retorted, "Oh, no! What good is a dress if one cannot even see it? No! Her dress must be such that a person would immediately see how we love and cherish our goddess. We must get stuffs made of pure gold; we must decorate the dress with precious stones; we..."

"And bury under that golden bark the beauty of our goddess? No!" exclaimed the third group. "We need silk – delicate, tender, flexible, obeying her every movement."

"Wool drapes better than silk," said others, and a heated discussion started. So passed the day.

In the meantime, the Brahmins again closed the temple of Trimurti, burned two widows on funeral pyres, and gave orders to prepare the procession with the statue of the god Indra.

The next day, a crowd of worshippers came to the goddess. Some brought many-colored shawls and tried them on her. "Look! How well they looks!"

Others yelled, "Away with your shawls! She needs a dress of brocade!" A third group carried laces, the fourth, precious stones. People argued, swore, and fought – about how the goddess should be shown to the world.

The Brahmins went ahead with their solemn procession

around the town, crushing to death the people who threw themselves under the wheels.

"And so it continues to this day," the fakir, who had not opened his mouth for thirty years, finished his story. "Everything remains as before. And the new goddess, well, they are still trying new gowns on her in order to show her to the world at her best!"

Translated by Rowen Glie

The Dream of a Hindu

Once upon a time, a very poor Hindu, who worked as a woodcutter, a laundry man, a coolie, a stone mason, or an elephant driver, as the circumstances dictated, fell asleep and had a wonderful dream. He dreamed of an enormous meadow covered with flowers that he had never seen before and which emitted heavenly scents. Walking toward him on this flower-strewn carpet with strides so light that her feet barely touched the petals was a wondrous woman whose eyes shone as two suns. Under her glances new flowers of extraordinary beauty sprouted. Her breath turned to jasmine, and a rain of falling petals. By the lotus flowers that were blooming in her hair, the poor Hindu immediately recognized her as the good goddess Parvati, the wife of the divine Siva, and overwhelmed by the blinding blaze of her eyes, he prostrated himself before her.

"Get up, Hindu!" said the goddess, and with the sound of her voice, the scent of flowers in the air became even stronger, and in the mouth of the Hindu there was a sweet taste as if he had just eaten some ginger jam. "Get up, Hindu," repeated the goddess. "Did you not, with a pure heart, bring flowers to the altar? Did you not give charity to poor people living in the temple? And the charity you offered was from the few rupees that you earned from very hard work. Did you not, in moments of leisure, love to sit under the sacred Bo tree, the very tree under which inspiration came to Buddha, and did you not, while sitting under this tree, meditate about divinity? Have you ever killed a fly or a mosquito or a gnat? Have you ever beaten the elephant you drove? Have you ever resisted when you yourself were beaten? Even when you were hungry, have you ever killed one of God's creatures for its meat? You did not even say a word to the 'gentleman' who beat you till your wounds bled because you had accidentally pushed him while carrying a load that was too heavy for you. Why then do not you dare to look straight into the eyes of your goddess?"

"No!" said the Hindu, "I have never done anything that is forbidden. But the light from your eyes blinds me."

"Rise, Hindu!" said the goddess. "The light from my eyes blinds only the weak, for the good it shines with a soft light."

The Hindu rose and the light from the eyes of the goddess was like the quiet radiance of the stars.

"You have never done anything that is forbidden," said the goddess with a kind smile, and from her smile magnificent pink lotuses blossomed. "Now Trimurti has summoned you before him so that you may see eternal life before seeing eternal rest.

The poor Hindu appeared before the three thrones of Trimurti, in which, surrounded by plumes of aromatic smoke, sat Brahma the creator, Vishnu the preserver, and Siva the destroyer.

"I gave him life," said Brahma, "and he never used it to take another creature's life."

"I gave him reason," said Siva, the master of fire. "I inserted a blazing ember in his head and he did not use his thought for plotting evil against his enemies."

Seeing the stripes of ashes on the forehead of the poor Hindu, the black Vishnu recognized the Hindu as one of his worshipers and said, "He is mine – he worshiped me!" And Vishnu touched the head of the poor Hindu so tenderly that it was as if he truly were a beloved son.

Vishnu called his wife Sarasvati, the all-knowing goddess of learning, and told her, "Take this Hindu, guide him, and show him eternal life in the same way that our priests show the temple to foreigners. The goddess Sarasvati, the beautiful goddess with a severe and serious face, touched the face of the Hindu lightly with her sword, sharp as a piece of broken glass. The Hindu then saw himself flying in endless space and he heard divine music which resembled singing to the sounds of countless violins. The melody was so exquisite that one could listen to it for centuries; it was the harmony of the universe, sung by beautiful worlds ringing the ether. Four fixed stars shone at the four sides of the universe. The bright star, lit by white light, sparkling like a diamond, was the star Dretoreastre, the star of the radiant South. The star burning with black fire like a black pearl, the pearl of the crown of Trimurti, was Viruba, the star of the West. The pink one, like the lightest of rubies, was Pakshi, the star of the East. And yellow, like the rarest of golden diamonds, was the star Yaisrevona, the star of the North. On each of these stars, frolicking like children and playing children's games, were fully grown people whose eyes were shining with purity and joy like the eyes of babies. "These are the righteous ones from the North, South, East, and West," said the stern and prophetic goddess Sarasvati,

"Everyone who followed the commandments of Trimurti and never committed a wicked act."

"And where are … the others?" the Hindu dared to ask.

The goddess cut the space with her sword, and the poor Hindu felt fear and shrank back. "Do not be afraid, you are with me!" said Sarasvati.

From a fiery abyss filled with snakes, a huge cobra standing on her tail rose toward them. She was hissing and licking herself with her forked tongue. Her eyes were burning with lust. She continued to rise, as if she were preparing to spring. Her throat was pulsating like a smith's bellows and it was glittering with all the colors of the spectrum. Her breath was coming hot like the sun's rays at noon in summer, and it seemed to the poor Hindu that her twisting and sparkling tongue would, at any moment, dart down and lick his feet. By her eyes which instilled fear and by her glances which petrified and paralyzed a man's hands and feet, the Hindu recognized in the cobra Iraideti, the terrible wife of the ruler of Hell. Her husband, the terrible three-eyed Purnak, sat on a blazing bonfire watching his son Athrit, a disgusting monster with a goat's beard, as he turned sinners into scorpions, toads, snakes and other evil creatures. With each new abomination from the hands of Athrit, Purnak would shout a joyful "Yes!"

"And how long will they suffer, these unfortunates?" asked the Hindu, pointing at the newly created reptiles.

"Until, by their suffering, they redeem their crimes and until they buy with their deaths the peace of non-being," replied the prophetic Sarasvati. And again she cut the space with her sword.

Now the Hindu was lying in a thick forest, on the edge of a small swamp with crystal clear water, under the shadow of a tall ornate fern. A lotus was bending over his head pouring an aroma from its cup and whispering to him, "I was a true and loving wife to my husband. I lovingly nursed only his children. My eyes troubled many, this is the truth, but no gold coins, no precious stones offered me by foreigners, or flowers which, as to a goddess, the Hindus would bring to me, could make me caress any man not my husband. I also wished to adorn my toes with sparkling rings, to wear glittering rings in my nose and ears, and to drape my body in silks. But to protect myself from sinful stares, I made do with a piece of rough white cotton. Never did my husband hear a bad word from me and always caresses awaited him in his house. I was the wife of a poor woodcutter and I was transformed into the best of flowers. Pick me and put me on the altar of Buddha. My aroma, like a scented prayer, will rise up to him, and my soul will fly away to Nirvana to be lost in the rapture of peace."

"We were young girls who never knew sinful caresses!" the jasmines said from their tree. "Pick us, so that we too might fly to Nirvana where, in divine peace, Buddha sleeps. Buddha does not hear or see anything; only the prayer-like scent of flowers can reach him."

The Hindu rose from the ground in wonder. In the bog of crystal clear water grew a tremendous flower of exquisite unearthly beauty. "Victoria Regia," foreigners called it. "I am the soul of a powerful queen whose subjects enjoyed only peace. The word 'war' was never used in my kingdom and I never uttered the word 'death'."

The whole forest was filled with whispers. Among tall and slender coconut palms and powerful breadfruit trees grew luxuriant banana trees. The young shoots of bamboo rustled as they told fairytales. From the knotty branches of a huge bamboo, shoots touched the ground and greedily drank its water. Palms resembling open peacock tails silently rocked back and forth like enormous fans. In the thickets, glittering like precious stones, insects played. Huge butterflies darted from branch to branch and sparkled with all the colors of the rainbow when they opened their wings. The apes shrieked as they swung from lianas which, like thick ropes, were thrown over the trees from one palm to another. Fast lizards ran about and a chameleon flashed, changing its color from blue to bright red. A huge shaggy spider spread its strong-as-steel web between trees and hid himself, waiting for the minuscule birds with little golden crests and tails that chirped carefree while hopping from bush to bush. A scorpion twisted its body and flashed close to the Hindu's feet without touching him.

All these creatures spoke in human language. "Cursed be my former life!" The hairy spider growled. "A lot of treasures were brought to me. I was the owner of a big manufacturing plant and I came from a far-off land, from an island where there is always cold and fog. How many Hindus spit blood from the beatings I gave them and how many of their wives, daughters, and sisters did I buy. And now, I am forced to suck the blood of little birds as I did of the poor Hindus. It would be much better if someone would kill me!"

"We were poor childless Hindus," said the palm and the banana trees, "and this is why we now grow in the thick woods. If we had had children, we would grow close to their houses, giving them sweet fruits and treats."

"I was always striving for the sky," said a Hindu who had been turned into a coconut palm.

"And I never harmed anyone, even though I used to have very worldly thoughts," said a cheerful banana tree.

A palm, swaying to and fro like a tremendous fan, rustled its leaves. "Look at me, traveler, how beautiful I am! All my life I helped the ones who needed help. No wonder the Hindus called me 'The Traveler's Palm.' Are you dying from thirst and heat? Break one of my leaves. Water, cold as ice and clear as crystal, is hidden there."

"Look into my eyes!" whispered a cobra, slithering out from under a fern. "Look at me, for I will not hurt you. Look into my eyes and see how many charms are hidden in them. You cannot tear your eyes from them. They were always like that, even when I was a woman, the wife of a Hindu just like you. I loved songs and dances, pretty clothes, gold and precious stones. And I had them. And now, everyone runs away from me, for I am the most dreadful of all reptiles and I seek human blood for Aichivori, my fearful mistress. There is no blood in Aichivori. She is lying as pale and blue as a corpse. I find a sleeping man and I bite him, and then I crawl to Aichivori and lick her lips with my forked tongue. Then Aichivori, the terrible, pale blue vampire, rises on the wings of a bat, flies to the cadaver, and starts to drink the dead man's blood, drop by drop, through the wound that I made with my poisonous teeth. Then the heart of Aichivori, filled with blood, causes a sinful blushing to appear on her pale cheeks. Passion overcomes her reasoning, and she flies to her master, Purnak, and caresses him in an abominable embrace. From these caresses are born scorpions and female vampires."

Two fires flashed in the darkness of the forest – a black panther snapped her teeth, howled, and leapt away to look for human flesh. The soul of a murderer lives in her.

"O God! Why did I eat animal meat and kill to live?" moaned a boar, racket through the brush. "That is why I was turned into a swine, the most disgusting of all beasts."

"I was a bride, but died before my wedding night," whispered a mimosa, shyly closing her petals.

An ilang-ilang waved an aromatic wreath around the head of the Hindu... But just then the poor Hindu jumped up woken by a strong kick from a boot. "Asleep, you lazy canaille! Is it for nothing that I pay you ten pennies a day?" yelled his boss, Mr. John, who continued to beat him. The Hindu shook his head, rubbed his eyes to clear his head, and smiled in spite of the strong pain in his side. He smiled to his ancestors, who were floating up into the sky, smiled to the souls of young girls, the souls which bloomed and exhaled fragrance on the jasmine bushes.

"You dare to smile, you swarthy rascal!" yelled Mr. John. But the poor Hindu continued to smile as he resumed his work. He smiled as a man who knows something that others could not even suspect. He knew something that Mister John could not even imagine.

Translated by Rowen Glie

A Chicken

Written on the occasion of Leo Tolstoy's illness

This happened in India, where gods are closer to people than anywhere in the world. And their life-giving breath produces miracles on earth. One such miracle occurred in Punjab.

Once there lived in Punjab a great Raja, wise and glorious. His fame spread from the Ganges to the Indus. Even in very distant lands they could sense the fragrance of his wisdom. People from far-off places came to listen to his wise thoughts. God himself descended from Heaven to talk to him. And thus God's word reached the people through him. The Raja received all visitors sitting in the shade of a spreading baobab. He was rich and powerful, but one day he gave up everything and retired into the woods so as to live far away from people and closer to the gods. All day long he would kneel on the ground looking up at the sky in rapture. In the azure enamel of the sky he could discern God's sad and kindly face looking down at the earth with love and sorrow. Whenever someone visited the old Raja he would interrupt his meditations and talk to them for as long as they wished. Anyone could come to the sage with their questions and doubts.

Wars raged everywhere on earth, violence was committed, and the world abounded in grief. Like an echo the old Raja responded to all the misfortunes from the depths of the woods where he suffered and prayed. His voice either thundered like a storm from the Heavens or flew over flowers like a light breeze in spring. He was severe toward the strong and loving toward the weak. And so he came to be known in India as "Great Conscience."

The old Raja lived as a hermit in the depths of the woods, having rejected all the joys of the world. He had enemies who asked accusingly:

"Why did he leave the world rather than live as befits a Raja?"

"He did it for the sake of fame!"

"That's sheer hypocrisy!"

"He's become fed up with everything."

But even worse than his enemies were his disciples. They also gave up everything, though they did not have much to give up. They also rejected everything, though there was nothing much for them to reject. They also started living under nearby trees, usually baobabs, because the great teacher lived under one. They were dressed in rags disintegrating on their bodies. They crawled on their bellies in fear of squashing some tiny insect in the grass. Coming across an ant they stopped to let it pass lest they hurt it. They considered themselves holy men because they covered their mouths with their hands lest they unintentionally breathe in a small fly and so cause its death. In imitation of the great teacher they also knelt from morning till night looking skywards. But unlike their teacher who saw gods in the sky, they only saw the ends of their noses.

One day the learned Raja fell ill. People were confused, they feared that the world might be deprived of Great Conscience. And so they hurried to summon some Anglian doctors, imploring them: "Save our sage!"

The Anglian doctors consulted their wisdom and said:

"The old Raja is emaciated. Cook a chicken and give the broth to the patient. This will give him strength."

A chicken was brought immediately. But the fakirs cried out in wild voices, like a pack of howling jackals:

"What! Was it not he who gave his last grains of rice to the ants when we were all starving? Because in a hungry year the ants, too, are starving. Was it not he who preached: 'Thou shalt not kill'. And you want to feed his heart with blood! To kill a living creature in order to save him!"

"But he will die!"

"We cannot allow murder!"

And so the old Raja died so that the chicken might live.

In great mysterious India gods live close to the earth. Having observed what happened, Magadewa smiled a sad smile and scored over the command he had earlier written on a gold plate: "Do not worship idols…" In its place he inscribed: "Do not worship chickens…"

Translated by Nathalie Roy

Complete GLAS backlist

Asar Eppel, *The Grassy Street.* Life in a Moscow suburb in the 1940s
Peter Aleshkovsky, *Skunk: A Life*. Bildungsroman set in today's
    Northern Russian countryside

ANTHOLOGIES

War & Peace, army stories versus women's stories: a compelling
    portrait of post-post-perestroika Russia
Captives. Victors turn out to be captives on conquered territory
Strange Soviet Practices. Stories and documentaries illustrating
    inimitably Soviet phenomena
NINE of Russia's Foremost Women Writers. Collective
    portrait of women's writing today
Childhood. The child is father to the man
Beyond the Looking-Glas, Russian grotesque revisited
A Will & a Way, women's writing of the 1990s
Booker Winners & Others-II. Samplings from the Booker
    winners of the early 1990s
Love Russian Style. Russia tries decadence
Booker Winners & Others. Mostly provincial writers
Jews & Strangers. What it means to be a Jew in Russia
Bulgakov & Mandelstam. Earlier autobiographical stories
Love and Fear. The two strongest emotions dominating Russian life
Women's View. Russian woman bloodied but unbowed
Soviet Grotesque. Young people's rebellion against the
    establishment
Revolution. The 1920s versus the 1980s

THE DEBUT SUBSERIES FOR YOUNG AUTHORS

Squaring the Circle. Winners of Debut
Mendeleev Rock, two short novels from Debut
Off the Beaten Track. Stories by Russian Hitchhikers.
Arslan Khasavov, *SENSE*, a novel about political struggles
    among young Russians today

BOOKS ABOUT RUSSIA

A.J. Perry, *Twelve Stories of Russia: A Novel, I guess*
Contemporary Russian Fiction: Russian authors interviewed by
    Kristina Rotkirch
Michele Berdy, The Russian Word's Worth. A humorous and
    informative guide to the Russian language, culture and translation